A
SHELTERING
TREE

Mary Ann Whitley

Walker and Company
New York, New York

The town of Milltown is real but all characters in this book are fictional and any resemblance to persons living or dead is purely coincidental.

Copyright © 1985 by Mary Ann Whitley

First published in the United States of America in 1985 by the Walker Publishing Company, Inc.

Published simultaneously in Canada by John Wiley & Sons Canada, Limited, Rexdale, Ontario.

Lyrics to "Stardust" by Hoagy Carmichael and Mitchell Parish. Copyright © 1929 by Mills Music, Inc. Copyright renewed. Used with permission. All Rights Reserved.

Library of Congress Cataloging in Publication Data

Whitley, Mary Ann.
    A sheltering tree.

    Summary: A thirteen-year-old girl living in a small country town determines to get away from her abusive stepfather and find the sister she hasn't seen in eight years.
    [1. Stepfathers—Fiction.   2. Family problems—Fiction.
3. Country life—Fiction]   I. Title.
PZ7.W5916Sh   1985   [Fic]   84-27100
ISBN 0-8027-6587-4

Printed in the United States of America

Book design by Teresa M. Carboni

10 9 8 7 6 5 4 3 2 1

A SHELTERING TREE

For Chris and Priscilla

"Friendship is a sheltering tree."

—Samuel Taylor Coleridge

One

LACEY Foster was in the chicken house shelling corn. She crouched there in the dim light, ripping the kernels fiercely off the cob and throwing them to the chickens. It made her fingers hurt to shell the corn like that, but she was angry, and it made her feel better to do something fast and hard.

She wished the freight train would come rushing through Milltown. It would rumble and roar so loud she could scream and no one would hear her. If it was a long train, its thunder would go on and on as it raced through the valley, across Blue River and out into the countryside again, the sound reverberating off the hills.

Right then, as she knelt in the chicken house, Lacey decided three things. One, she would never speak to Lonzie again. Two, she was going to leave home as soon as she could. Three, she was going to find her sister, Vernal. She had stopped shelling the corn for a moment and the chickens greedily pecked at the edge of her shoe, searching for more. She went back to her task and threw out another handful.

The first part wouldn't be so hard, Lacey told herself.

Lonzie wasn't her *real* father, anyway. His last name, Jackson, was different from hers. Her mother had married him only to make things easier on herself, trying to raise two kids alone. At least, that's what she said. It was a long time ago and Lacey really couldn't remember much about it, except that after the wedding at the courthouse, she had cried and cried because Lonzie was sending her sister, Vernal, away.

Shreds of memory came back to her, and she ripped harder at the ear of corn. Lonzie and her mother had walked down the big stone steps of the courthouse, with Lacey and Vernal trailing behind. Lacey was five and Vernal was eight. Her sister had held her hand securely, protectively.

"Adelle, we'll wait till tomorrow to take Vernal," Lonzie had said. His voice was unfeeling, lean, and hard like his tall, thin frame. Her mother was thin, too, but in a soft, almost frail way. Her brown hair hung loosely about her face in gentle waves.

A look of shock had registered on her mother's face and she whispered, pleading, half-turning away from Lacey and Vernal, "Just give things a little time. It won't be so hard, you'll see."

She had acted like she didn't want the children to hear what she was saying, but Vernal and Lacey heard every word.

"I aim to do what I said and I don't want to hear any more from you," Lonzie had said. "I won't support two kids that ain't even mine."

The two sisters hung back. Lacey could still feel the panic rising. She could still remember how she'd wished she could take her sister's hand and run far away. Instead, she had stood as if planted on those cold stone steps, clutching Vernal's hand even harder. She looked up into her sister's face and saw tears running from her clear blue eyes. But Vernal never made a sound. Lacey realized she could hardly remember what her sister looked like after all these years; she was thirteen now, so Vernal must be sixteen.

Lacey stopped her shelling for a minute and shut her eyes. Vernal was slender, like their mother, with white skin and ice blue eyes. Her hair was straight and thin, like Lacey's, but it was almost white. Lacey's was brown. Vernal was so delicate and pale-looking that people called her "China Doll."

That night, Lacey and Vernal had slept close together, as if holding one another tightly could prevent Lonzie from separating them. They'd heard Lonzie and their mother arguing and Lonzie saying, "She's the oldest, she has to go."

In the morning, Vernal was gone, leaving an empty feeling that seemed to grip Lacey's insides. How could their mother have done this?

For a long time Lacey thought Vernal was staying with some relatives, because her mother said Vernal had been sent to a foster home.

"Are those Fosters our relatives?" Lacey used to ask.

"No, honey, they're not."

"Can't we go see Vernal?" she'd ask.

"No, honey. I don't know where she is."

Her mother's eyes would get watery when Lacey asked questions like those. That frightened her, so she soon learned not to ask anymore.

Lacey guessed she had hated Lonzie since that day at the courthouse.

She threw down some more corn and the chickens pecked eagerly at it. Outside, the honeysuckle growing up the side of the henhouse gave off a thick, sweet scent.

Lonzie had done other things to hurt her. Tonight was only the latest episode, but it had made her resolve to do something about it.

The past eight years had been full of incidents that had deepened her anger. She could feel it building inside her, and she knew it would burst sooner or later, just as a dark storm cloud would inevitably let loose the rain it held inside.

The year after Lonzie had married her mother, he had forced her to sell the golden oak dresser and the sturdy rocking chair that had belonged to Lacey's grandmother.

They had needed money that month to pay some bills. Lacey begged her mother not to let him sell the furniture. She remembered being comforted in that rocking chair when she was very small. And she loved to rub her fingers over the smooth surface of the dresser. It seemed to Lacey that the dresser and the chair were the only things left from her old life—before Vernal had been taken away.

Lacey had been so upset about the furniture that finally her mother had said to Lonzie, "Now you promised me after the wedding you'd not spend so much money at the tavern. If you'd kept your promise we wouldn't need anything extra now."

"No one's going to tell me how I spend the money. Especially since *I'm* the one who's making it!" Lonzie retorted. "I especially don't take orders from a six-year-old kid who's not even mine," he'd said, pushing Lacey across the room so hard that she fell on her knees in a corner.

Without saying any more, he had carried the dresser and the chair out to his pickup truck and had driven away with them. What he did with the money he got from selling them, Lacey never knew.

Lonzie had never changed. Each month it was a struggle for her mother to find money to pay the bills after he finished spending half of it at the tavern. Other conflicts began when Lacey started school. Each time her mother showed Lonzie a drawing Lacey had made in school, he'd criticize it and say, "We'll just see how far that gets you when you're out of school."

Now Lacey usually hid her drawings from Lonzie. She knew he'd never say anything good about them, so she might as well not show them to him.

Even so, she had felt good when she had come home today. She had brought a folder of drawings from school. She laid them on the kitchen table on purpose because she was proud of them. She didn't care what Lonzie thought. She was especially proud of the sketch she'd made of the Snows' field with the horses running through it. She loved to capture their grace and elegance. When she put it down on paper, she felt like she was running along with the horses.

"That's really pretty, Lacey," her mother had said as she set three plates on the table for supper. She picked up the sketch, handling the paper gingerly, as if her touch would damage it somehow. Her expression softened and she smiled as she laid it back on the table.

Then Lonzie came in and dropped his big lean frame into the chair. It creaked when he sat down. Lacey could tell he was angry and she wished now she hadn't put the pictures on the table where he would see them right away. Lonzie would surely make some comment.

He took off his shirt. It was covered with limestone dust from the quarry and it rose in a fine white cloud around him, then settled on the floor. His dark hair was streaked with the dust too. Lacey smelled beer on his breath—that odor meant he was liable to be in a bad mood.

Her mother set a plate of beans and another of cornbread down on the table. "Did you find out about overtime?" Her voice was cautious.

"Overtime?" Lonzie said in a mocking tone. "Won't be any overtime work now. Quarry's cuttin' back. Road-building money got cut by the state, so they don't need so much concrete. And if they don't need concrete, they don't need lime."

He looked up as if challenging her mother to argue. But, as always, she was sitting quietly, not looking at him.

"So that's the way it goes," Lonzie said. "You give 'em your life and that's the reward you get—soon as work drops off, you drop off. Snow's never gonna give us nothin' but these houses to live in, and even then they call it Snow's Row."

He slapped butter on the hot cornbread and licked his greasy fingers.

"What're these pictures doing here on the supper table?" Lonzie demanded.

"Lacey made them at school. Aren't they nice?" her mother asked. Her tone said she was trying to make Lonzie forget he was angry.

"Pictures won't get you anywhere. Nothin' but a waste of time."

Lonzie shoved the papers off the table with his greasy fingers and they fell under his chair. He pushed them away with his foot. Lacey felt like part of her had been pushed off the table and stepped on, too. She never said a word but she felt the anger rising higher and higher until she was sure it would explode right out of her head. Then she pushed her chair back and stood up.

"I'm gonna feed the chickens," she announced and walked out the door into the back yard, across the grass and into the chicken house without looking back.

"Since when are you so helpful?" Lonzie called, but Lacey ignored him.

"Lonzie, now, it's nothing. . . ." she heard her mother's voice begin.

Lacey kept on shelling the corn, thinking how those pictures were under Lonzie's chair and his shoes had probably made big dirty smudges on them. She could never forgive him about Vernal. This was just one more thing added to the list of things she couldn't forgive. But there had been too many, and there could only be more. That was why she never wanted to speak to him again. And that was also why she was going to leave home. That would be a little harder, and it might take time. But she could do it if she planned it right. And the third thing—finding her sister. She didn't want to think about how hard that might be. When she went back into the house, the supper dishes had been cleared away and her pictures were gone. She didn't ask her mother about them.

Two

THE next morning, like she did every school day, Lacey walked two doors down to her friend Callie's house so they could walk to school together. Lacey's stomach still churned with last night's anger as she walked along. Why couldn't she have a regular family like Callie's? Callie was waiting for Lacey on her front porch and came out to meet her.

They fell into step together as they walked past the row of little white houses. The houses were owned by Snow's quarry and most of the workers rented them. They looked nearly identical. Callie's house looked a little different, though, because her father had bought it from the Snows. He'd saved up enough money to buy it and when he did, they put pretty blue shutters on it and Callie's mother planted geraniums in the yard beneath the front windows. Lacey sometimes envied Callie for her looks, too. She was slim, but not thin; taller than Lacey but not ungainly. Her hair was a rich shade of brown, not drab and mousy-colored.

"I'm going to leave home," Lacey announced.

"You mean run away? When?"

"No, I don't mean run away. I mean leave. If you run away, they bring you back. When I go, it's for good."

"Oh," said Callie. "How will you do it?"

"I don't know exactly yet. But I won't have to live with Lonzie anymore, that's the important thing."

"What did Lonzie do?"

"He ruined the drawings I brought home yesterday. It's never gonna get any better. And I want to find Vernal."

"How long ago did your father send her away?" Callie inquired.

"You mean how long ago did *Lonzie* send her away. Lonzie's not my father."

Callie took offense. "Well, you don't know who your *real* father is, do you?"

"No. So what?"

"Well, since you live with Lonzie he might as well be your father."

"No, he can't be," Lacey said fiercely. "And he never will be. I don't want him to be."

Callie shrugged and they walked in silence the rest of the way to the schoolhouse that stood at the end of Snow's Row. The red brick building was old, shaded by large maple trees that had been planted years ago when the school had been built.

At lunch that day, as they always did, Callie and Lacey sat on the rock wall that ran around the schoolyard under a big leafy maple tree. A chain link fence had been erected atop the wall to make a taller enclosure. Honeysuckle draped itself along the wire, the blooms perfuming the air. Callie unwrapped her lunch.

"Want a piece of my cornbread? I have two."

"No!" Lacey said more abruptly than she had intended. Cornbread just reminded her of Lonzie's greasy fingers touching her drawings. Callie didn't seem to notice her tone.

"You know, Lace, if you want to leave home, why don't you just wait a few years and drop out of school and get married. That's what I'm gonna do."

Lacey stared at her, unbelieving, as if she'd been betrayed. "I wouldn't be any better off than I am now. I'd end up being in the same fix my mother is. I'm not going to let that happen to me." Lacey picked at her sandwich, tearing off bits of crust and eating them.

"Well . . ." Callie said. "I don't think it would be so bad. Just be careful who you pick."

"Oh, Cal, sometimes you just don't understand!"

How could she explain she wanted something different from what her mother had. Her mother was stuck with Lonzie and there didn't seem to be any way out. When she thought about that, she felt hopeless, as if she were drowning, being sucked into a whirlpool in the river, farther and farther until she didn't even feel like fighting it. She hated that feeling and it was part of the reason she wanted to get away. She didn't want to live forever feeling like that.

The school bell rang and the students filed back inside the building. The teacher came up to Lacey's desk that afternoon and said, "Did you take your drawings home yesterday, Lacey?"

"Yes, ma'am."

"Oh, I see." She paused. Lacey wondered if she'd done something wrong. "I was going to ask if you might bring them back so I could put them up on the wall here. I like the one of the horses in the field. I can understand if your parents want them, they're lovely . . ."

"No, they don't want them," Lacey said, looking down at her desk and lining up her pencils along the edge of it. "But I can't bring you the picture. It got ruined. Lonzie stepped on it . . . accidentally."

"Oh," the teacher said. "I'm sorry. Maybe you can draw another one sometime."

"Yeah," Lacey said. She could draw it again, she thought. The same horses running in the same field. But this time she wouldn't leave it around for Lonzie to see. She wasn't going to speak to him, anyway.

After school, Lacey and Callie walked down to the bridge over Blue River. It was getting warm enough now, as spring moved closer to summer, to walk out on the dam, sit on the foot-wide concrete wall and dangle their feet in the water. The river level was low now, so it wasn't dangerous. But the water was almost too cold. They just dipped their toes in and out. The water curled and rippled around the big stone columns near the riverbank where the old mill had stood.

"Don't you wish they hadn't torn down the mill?" Lacey asked wistfully.

"I don't know. They say it was full of rats. And crazy old Hollis slept there," Callie said.

"Hollis never caused any trouble. He sleeps in the Snows' barn now, so what's the difference? Now Milltown doesn't even have a mill. Just this old dam, and part of it's falling down."

"Oh, gee, Lace, why do you make such a big deal out of it?"

"Because it's sad, somehow. Because it would be nice to see what this town looked like when things were going good. The quarry's not even much now. About all that's left is the river."

Lacey plunged her feet into the water, all the way up to her ankles, splashing water on Callie's legs.

"Why'd you do that? It's cold!" Callie exclaimed.

"I'm sorry," Lacey said sharply. "Let's go." She felt ashamed that she had acted angrily toward Callie without any explanation.

They walked barefoot halfway home until their feet dried, then stopped and put on their shoes. They parted at Lacey's house.

"I'll see you tomorrow, Cal," Lacey said.

When she went inside, her mother was setting the table for supper. "Lacey, honey, would you burn the trash and feed the chickens?"

Lacey carried the paper bag out to the wire trash bin. She shook the contents out, knelt and lit a match to it. She stood up, watching the flames take hold and caught sight of a familiar piece of paper. But it was too late to pull it out of the fire. The flames seared the paper, blackening and curling it as they moved over the drawing, over the graceful horses running across the field, and darkened the smudge from Lonzie's shoe. The blaze flared and the drawing was gone.

A choking feeling gripped Lacey's throat. She went into the chicken house. It was dark there and no one would see her cry and the chickens' clucking would keep anyone from hearing her.

She cried while she shelled the corn furiously. The chickens didn't care. But she realized she'd have to go back in the house and she didn't want her eyes to look red. Lacey tried to calm herself and forget her anger. She tried to keep her head down when she went back in, but her mother saw her face anyway.

"Lacey, what's wrong?"

Lacey just shook her head, looking down at the floor. "I'm okay."

Her mother sighed, setting a jar of pickled beets on the table. "I wish you'd tell me what's hurtin' you."

Lacey kept the tears down and went into her room. She sat on the edge of the bed. If she pretended there was nothing to be upset about, she would be all right. Just push the pain away, down deep inside, she told herself. Lonzie especially would never know that throwing her sketches away had hurt her.

Lacey kept her promise to herself and never said a word to Lonzie all the way through dinner. He didn't notice that she hadn't spoken until he asked her how school was. Lacey looked down at her plate and shrugged.

"I asked how was school?" he repeated. Lacey just shrugged again. She wouldn't look at him.

"Oh, for God's sake," he said disgustedly. "I guess she's deaf and dumb."

"Just let her be, Lonzie." Lacey's mother gave him a pleading look and they finished the meal in silence.

Three

THE next week was hot. All the trees were deep green and haze hung over the hills, making them look pale blue in the distance. Callie came for her after school.

"Want to go swimming? Let's go down to the bridge."

"Okay, but just a minute. I want to get something." Lacey ran to her bedroom and got her sketchpad, which she had hidden under her pillow.

"What's that for?" asked Callie as they walked down the street.

"I'm just going to do some drawing."

"Oh, cripe, that's just like homework," Callie said. "Come on, leave it home."

"No, I'm not going to," Lacey said firmly.

Callie shrugged and said no more. The heat rose off the asphalt as they walked down to the bridge. The water was already filled with swimmers and the gravel lot next to the bait shop was crowded with cars belonging to out-of-towners.

They walked up the river, back from the bridge, until they found a quiet spot. They sat on the bank and dangled their feet in the water. The earth where they sat was damp and smelled slightly fishy, like river mud.

"Are you going in?" Callie said, as she took off her shoes and tossed them onto the grass.

"Not right now," Lacey said. She opened the sketchbook and gazed downstream. She started to draw the riverbank and the swimmers leaping off the bridge. Her pencil seemed to skim over the paper, sketching outlines, then returning to fill in the details and add shading. Her hand moved quickly as she bent over the paper, but it was relaxing. She felt like she was transferring her feelings all the way from her head through the pencil and onto the paper. That made her forget, for a while, about what Lonzie had done. She had even forgotten Callie was there with her.

"Lace! Come on! Come in for a while."

Lacey looked up with a jerk. She put down her pad and took off her shoes. She tiptoed down the bank, squishing brown mud between her toes. Then she eased herself down into the water. It was cold at first. Her shorts and blouse hung on her, wet and heavy.

They paddled around. Callie nudged Lacey.

"Look, Lace, there's old Hollis."

Hollis ambled down the riverbank with a paper bag clutched tightly in his hand. He stopped at the trash barrel behind the bait shop and began rooting through it. Glass and metal clinked against the sides of the rusty barrel.

"He's just hunting pop bottles to take to the store for money," Lacey said.

Callie crinkled her nose. "He's so strange. You'd think he'd get a job or something. How can he stand to go through garbage cans? I'd rather do just about anything than go through people's trash." Callie gave an exaggerated shudder.

Lacey watched Hollis's hunched form as he bent over the barrel, intent on his task. Everything about him seemed worn and faded. He always wore the same gray trousers, tennis shoes that had holes in the toes and a faded red baseball cap. His hair was sandy so it was hard to guess his age; he wasn't really old but he was well into middle age. His gray eyes were pale and vacant. He never spoke. As long as Lacey could remember, she'd seen Hollis walking up and down the streets, picking up bottles, poking through garbage cans.

"My mother said he got kind of simpleminded years ago, after his sister killed herself. That was all the family he had left and he didn't have any money, so he just took to sleeping in the old mill. Until they tore it down," Lacey said.

"I've heard that before. My mother says he's just plain crazy and to stay away from him. I guess he'll stay in the Snows' barn until they tear *it* down," Callie said and stood up to go ashore. She squeezed water out of her blouse. "I don't know why the Snows let him stay there."

"I guess the Snows aren't that low-down to throw somebody like Hollis out on the street," Lacey said.

Lacey felt pity toward the odd man. She had felt so lonely when Vernal was taken away, but she couldn't imagine how much worse it must feel to have no one at all. No wonder he was off in the head. Sometimes, however, she thought maybe things would have been easier if Vernal *had* died. Then she'd *know* she'd never have a chance to see her sister again. The way it was now, she was always filled with a vague hope and longing that never quite went away. She picked her sketchpad up off the damp riverbank. Maybe tomorrow she'd draw a picture of Hollis wandering along the river.

Four

A boy sat across the schoolroom from Lacey. Thin and frail with unruly straw-colored hair and dark eyes, he looked at her and smiled, as if they were sharing some humorous story, as if they'd known each other for a long time.

Lacey had never seen him before but she smiled back.

Today was art class—they had it two times a week. The art teacher, Mrs. Baxter, said they could leave their desks and use the big worktables at the back of the room. The boy came over and sat down across from Lacey. She smiled again and started sketching a horse. He looked at it, upside down, from across the table.

Lacey's hand moved effortlessly across the paper, her pencil quickly capturing the graceful curves of the animal's arched neck with a strong, sure stroke. Then, with a more delicate pressure, she added a waving, flowing mane. It was easy to lose herself in the creation of the image. It seemed that what emerged on the paper was a part of her.

"I had a horse once," said the boy abruptly. Lacey looked up in surprise.

"What happened to it?" she asked.

"It died."

Before she could ask another question, he said, "It got run over."

Lacey laughed outright at that incongruous statement. "What do you mean, *run over*? You can't *run over* a horse."

"It got hit by a car. It got loose and ran out on the highway. The farmer who owned the farm took it and hooked the dead horse up to his tractor and dragged it up and down the pasture as an example to the other horses."

"That's crazy! The horses wouldn't understand what he was doing."

"Yeah, I know." He was silent for a minute and Lacey continued sketching. She was about to ask him if he was new in Milltown when he suddenly spoke up again.

"It was a real nice horse, you know? I used to stand out in the field and watch it. I'd talk to it. That horse understood me. I'd say things and it would nod its head."

Lacey wanted to laugh again but the boy's tone of voice was so serious, like he was confiding in her, that she couldn't. She couldn't bear to tell him it was impossible for a horse to know what he was saying. Instead she said, "Oh, sure, I think horses can understand you sometimes."

"I know there's a horse heaven somewhere and that horse went to heaven and then came back as a person. It was a smart horse, and I just know that's what happened. I believe that."

"Well," Lacey said. "That's what's important, that you believe it." She didn't know why she was going along with him. She didn't really believe him, but his sincerity was charming.

"You think so?" He just kept looking at her, those dark eyes bright and burning. He kept smiling, too, and that was disconcerting. Lacey glanced quickly down at her paper to avoid looking at him.

Then he said, "Have you ever just gotten down on the grass and eaten it the way a horse does?"

"No," Lacey said sarcastically. She decided to tease him. "I always pick my grass before I eat it." She looked at him to see if he'd laugh at her joke. But he went right on.

"I think it's neat, the way horses eat." Then he made a grand gesture, stretching his neck out longer and jerking his head from side to side like a horse pulling snatches of grass.

Lacey laughed at the ridiculous picture he made. He sat there, tilting his head to one side, a crooked smile on his face. He seemed to be waiting, gauging her reaction. She thought it was entirely possible he had fabricated the whole story about the horse. She didn't know how to take him.

"What's your name?" she asked.

"Christopher," he answered. "Christopher Curry."

Five

Lacey was getting ready to leave for school two days later when her mother came to the bedroom door.

"I think someone's waiting for you, out in the front yard," she said.

"Tell Callie to go on. I'll catch up."

"It's not Callie."

"Who is it?"

"I don't know."

Lacey went to the front door, still holding her hairbrush. She almost dropped it when she saw Christopher standing there, with a cluster of purple irises in his hand.

"I came to walk you to school. You look like someone who should be walked to school."

He thrust the irises at her, looking directly into her eyes, his mouth curving upwards on one side in that funny way, as he waited for her reaction.

Lacey was flustered. Still clutching the hairbrush in one hand, she took the purple flowers in the other.

"I can't take these to school," she blurted out. She rushed inside with the irises and stuffed them into a jar. She caught her mother's glance and felt her face turning pink with embarrassment. Then she hurried out of the house. Christopher walked beside her along the sidewalk, having to shorten his stride to match hers.

"Where do you live? You're new here, aren't you?" Lacey asked.

"Down by the river, on Back Street."

"Oh, that's where it floods when the river gets high. Which house do you live in?"

"The white one on the corner with the big front porch."

"But I thought that's where the McIntoshes live."

"It is. I'm living with them," Christopher said. "I'm a foster child."

Lacey laughed, covering her mouth, as she suddenly thought of a way to make a joke.

"What's so funny about it?"

"I'm a Foster child, too."

"You *are?*" Christopher's serious brown eyes turned on her with amazement. Lacey saw that he didn't understand her pun.

"Sure . . . my last name's Foster!"

Christopher grinned. "Well, we have more in common than I thought."

Lacey didn't ask him any more about being a foster child. That reminded her of Vernal . . . Vernal was probably a foster child now, if someone hadn't adopted her. Lacey didn't want to think about that too much. Every time she had tried to ask her mother about where Vernal was, she'd just say, "I'm sure she's in a good home. Don't worry yourself."

When they got to school, Lacey saw the other girls from her class staring at her as she walked up to the building with Christopher. She felt her face turn hot and was sure it was red again. All of a sudden she remembered Callie— she always walked to school with Callie! When Christopher came, she'd forgotten. She looked back toward the street. There was Callie walking quickly toward her. She knew she couldn't just leave Christopher standing there by himself, and she didn't really want to, either. She told him the truth.

"Here comes my friend Callie. I usually walk to school with her."

"She looks mad," Christopher said. "Maybe I should have picked *her* some flowers."

Callie walked right past Lacey and Christopher, giving them an angry scowl.

"Cal—wait—I'm sorry," Lacey said, but Callie brushed past her quickly.

Lacey couldn't get Callie to look at her the whole morning. They usually exchanged silent jokes and muffled laughs throughout the day, but today Callie never once looked up from her notebook.

Two can play this game, Lacey thought, and scribbled fiercely in her notebook. Why should Callie act so angry and treat her as if she weren't there? Was she jealous just because she'd walked to school with Christopher?

At lunch, in the schoolyard, Lacey confronted Callie.

"What's going on?"

"What are you talking about?" Callie asked sullenly.

"You know what I'm talking about. You've ignored me all day long."

"*You* didn't wait for me this morning. Do you remember anything about that? Do you remember walking to school with someone else?"

"Christopher . . ." Lacey started to say.

"Whoever he is. Everybody in school's talking about that strange kid. Nobody knows anything about him."

"Then how do you know he's strange?" Lacey countered.

"Never mind that, I suppose the fact that you didn't wait for me isn't your fault."

"It's just that I don't see what's wrong with being nice to someone," Lacey said in defense. "He's been nice to me so far."

They had walked to the edge of the schoolyard, where the other students couldn't hear what they were saying.

"Well, you're not being very nice to *me*," Callie snapped. "We always walk to school together, and this morning I show up and you're with this Christopher whoever-he-is."

"I swear, Callie, you act like you're jealous. Do you think you're not still my best friend?"

Callie answered lamely, "Well, how would you feel? . . ." and stared at the ground.

"I'm sorry, all right?" Lacey said.

The warning bell rang, signaling that the lunch period was over, and they walked briskly back toward the school.

That afternoon was art class again. Christopher was at the classroom door waiting for Lacey. When he saw her, he grinned. His hair looked rumpled, like he'd slept on it and got up without combing it. Maybe it always looked like that, no matter what he did.

"Did I get you in trouble?" he asked.

"In trouble?"

"With your friend."

"Oh, no, no. I told her I was sorry at lunchtime."

"Well . . ."

Christopher looked at her as if asking a silent question. Lacey suspected he wanted to ask her about walking to school together again.

"Maybe you'd better not wait for me tomorrow," Lacey said at last.

"Okay. I'll see you some other time."

They did some sketches in art class. Christopher drew crazy-looking people upside down on his paper so that from where she sat, across the table from him, their faces were looking at her. She couldn't help laughing and had to try to keep quiet. She could see the laughter in Christopher's eyes. It was as if he enjoyed entertaining her. Once Lacey noticed some of the kids at another table, giggling and whispering, and the thought crossed her mind briefly that they were making fun of her and Christopher. She waited until they were looking, then gave them an angry glance.

Callie was waiting for her when school let out, cutting between her and Christopher as they began walking toward home. Callie's expression told him he wasn't welcome. Christopher hung back.

"Bye," he said, and stood there, looking kind of awkward and out of place. Lacey felt a little twinge of anger at Callie. Why did she have to act so possessive?

"Let's go down to the dam," suggested Callie.

"Okay," Lacey agreed, but her voice was halfhearted. She felt a little empty, as if a space had opened up between them. Kind of like a crack starting in a patch of dry earth. She wanted to be with both Christopher and Callie—was there anything wrong with that?

They sat on the dam, their feet hanging down in the cool water. The river was low. There hadn't been any rain in a week, and the water barely trickled across the top of the dam.

Callie got right to the point. "All the kids are saying Christopher's kind of weird. He makes up stories. He doesn't hang around with the rest of the kids. Some of the other kids say he came here because there's something wrong with him, and his parents got rid of him."

"Why are you telling me things like that?" Lacey demanded.

Callie shrugged. "I'm just telling you."

"You're trying to say Christopher is weird or crazy or something. Maybe nobody's taken the time to get to know him."

"Oh, excuse *me*! If you know so much about him, what do you know?"

"For one thing," Lacey said, "he's a foster child like my own sister probably is right now, that's what."

Lacey sat staring down at the water, surprised that she had defended Christopher so forcefully. She had thought a lot about how lonely it must have been for Vernal. At least Lacey still had her own mother even if she did have a stepfather she hated. Now she realized she'd seen some of that pain and loneliness in Christopher's eyes, too. That must have been what struck her. Behind that smile, his eyes were dark and full of feeling. Lacey got up and walked across the cool, wet concrete on top of the dam.

Callie jumped up and splashed after her. "Lace, I'm sorry."

"Never mind. I just want to go home now, okay?"

"Walk to school together tomorrow?" Callie's voice was hesitant.

"Sure."

When Lacey got home, she found her mother had put the jar of irises on the kitchen table. She got her sketchpad and sat down to draw a picture of them. She wanted to capture their delicate curves on paper. When she'd finished, her mother said, "That's beautiful. Why don't we hang it up on the kitchen wall?"

"I don't know," Lacey hesitated. "I'm not done with it yet." She didn't want to see Lonzie rip it down or throw it away.

Lacey's mother began setting the table. "We'll go ahead and eat now. I don't know when he'll be home. I expect he has to work late. I'll just keep Lonzie's supper warm on the stove."

Lacey knew Lonzie wasn't really working late. Her mother had said that before, and Lacey knew it was usually an excuse to make all of them feel better. It was her way of saying Lonzie would probably stay out late drinking.

Lacey bit her lip to keep herself from saying anything. She wished her mother would just stand up to Lonzie and shout at him and tell him how hard things were because he spent his money at the tavern.

But that had only happened once and Lacey knew it would never happen again. The only time her mother had tried that was years ago, but it was as clear in Lacey's memory as if it had happened yesterday.

Loud voices had awakened Lacey one night and she lay there for a while, trying to figure out what Lonzie and her mother were arguing about. Her mother's voice was high and angry.

"We can't go on like this! You *promised* me you'd use this week's wages to pay off some of our bills. We owe Sam Tucker's store for two weeks' groceries. I'm ashamed to ask him for any more credit."

"Oh, Sam don't care. He knows he'll get his money," Lonzie answered.

"But you *promised* me, and tonight I come to find out you've gone and spent a big part of it drinking again—what you didn't lose at cards!"

"Next week'll be soon enough to pay those bills," Lonzie said. His voice was loud, but unsteady, like it was when he'd been drinking.

Lacey lay in her dark bedroom, watching the light under the bottom of the door and listening to their voices grow louder and louder.

"*Next* week we'll be even deeper in the hole!" her mother shouted. "If you don't want us sleeping in the street, you'd better make some changes."

There was a scraping of wood on wood, as if Lonzie had pushed his chair away from the table and stood up.

"You want some changes? Okay, I'll tell you what I can do—"

Lacey heard him striding across the floor and the next instant her bedroom door was flung open. Lonzie pulled her from the bed and out into the kitchen. Lacey was so scared she was shaking, and she squinted against the bright, hard light from the bare bulb on the ceiling.

"I'll tell you something that would make things a lot

easier around here," Lonzie said viciously. "One less mouth to feed. You want me to send *her* off like I did Vernal?" Lonzie held Lacey by the shoulders and shook her as he spoke.

Lacey's mother gasped and drew away from him.

"I don't *have* to provide for kids that ain't mine," Lonzie went on. "Just think about that for a minute."

Lacey began crying, half from fear and half from the pain of Lonzie's tight grasp. She didn't make any noise, though. She was too frightened.

Her mother had backed farther away from Lonzie. She bowed her head and clasped her hands together tightly. She almost looked like she was praying, Lacey thought. When her mother lifted her head, Lonzie met her eyes with a defiant gaze.

"Well, do you want that?" he taunted.

Lacey's mother shook her head. "No," she said in a voice that sounded tired and defeated.

"Fine," Lonzie said and released his hold on Lacey's shoulders.

Even now, Lacey flinched when she remembered how she'd recoiled from Lonzie's grasp.

She and her mother sat down at the table. They ate their supper quietly.

At last her mother said, "If I could sell a few more eggs every month, I could put a little money away. I need to get an electric light for the chicken house. With a light on, the chickens would lay through the winter. It wouldn't take much electricity."

Her mother went on as if she were rehearsing the speech she would make to Lonzie, convincing herself that it sounded like a good idea.

Six

THAT night Lacey lay awake in the dark, watching the pattern of moonlight through the trees wavering on her wall and listening to the night insects. She heard Lonzie come home finally, loudly getting undressed, thumping his shoes onto the floor.

She could hear her mother's voice, but it was barely loud enough to make out the words. There was no trouble hearing Lonzie's voice, though.

"You never made nothin' on them chickens anyway. What's wrong—don't I bring in enough? We're gettin' by all right, ain't we?"

Her mother's voice interrupted softly, then she was cut off again.

"Not running electricity out to that henhouse. Next thing you'll be wanting is a brand-new chicken house. I should have gotten rid of those chickens a long time ago."

Lacey sighed and turned over. She knew Lonzie wouldn't go along with any idea of her mother's. Then a bit later she heard a sound that wasn't quite like a bird outside the window. She got up and looked out. Someone was standing in the shadow of the big sycamore. The figure stepped away from the tree, and she could see that it was Christopher.

"What are you doing here?" she whispered.

"Waiting for you to get up and come outside."

"What?"

"Come on, get dressed. We're going for a midnight ride."

"But I can't leave. Lonzie would kill me if he found out," she whispered.

"Be really quiet," Christopher whispered back. "There's nothing to be afraid of."

Christopher gently pushed the window up and lifted out the screen so Lacey could climb through. The windows were tall and the sill was close to the floor so it was easy to step out. Lonzie and her mother's bedroom did not have a window on this wall of the house, so they wouldn't hear her.

Five minutes later, Lacey was walking fast to keep up with Christopher. They cut through the yards of houses on the streets behind Lacey's house.

"Where are we going?"

"To the Snows' farm."

Lacey couldn't figure out what he had in mind so she followed him. They came to the pasture fence. Christopher held the barbed wire so she could crawl under it without catching her shirt. Once they were under the fence, Lacey could see Mr. Snow's mares grazing in the field. They were dark, indefinite shapes moving through the moonlight in the grass. The farm was a big one, but it had once been bigger. The land where her house stood had once been part of it, but Mr. Snow had parceled the land into lots. Some he had sold; on others, he had built houses to rent to the quarry workers. That was Snow's Row.

Christopher began running lightly through the wet grass.

"Where are you going?" Lacey called to him between gasps of breath as she tried to keep pace.

"To the barn, to get a bridle."

"You're going to ride one of Mr. Snow's horses?"

"That's the idea."

"But you can't go in there—that's where Hollis stays!" Lacey exclaimed. She'd always felt sorry for Hollis. But now a little shiver of fear passed over her. She wasn't sure how he'd react if he encountered someone in the barn at night. Maybe Callie's mother was right and they should stay away from him.

"Just wait here," Christopher reassured her.

Lacey tried to stay close to the side of the barn in the shadows. She could see lights in the Snows' house a few hundred feet away. Christopher reappeared silently with a bridle slung over his shoulder. He headed back out to the pasture, walking confidently as if he had done this a dozen times.

He plucked some clover and walked right up to one of the mares. She was dark brown—at least she looked dark brown in the moonlight—with a white patch on her forehead. She came forward as if expecting the tidbit. As the mare lipped the sweet leaves from his palm, Christopher slipped the reins over her head and slid the bit into her mouth, all in one deft motion.

"You sure act like you know what you're doing," Lacey observed.

"I told you, I had a horse once."

"Oh, I forgot. The one that got run over, right?"

Christopher laughed. He led the mare over to the fence, scrambled up on a post and slid over onto her back.

"Well, maybe I did make up *that* part. But I *did* have a horse that was practically mine once, and I used to ride it every day . . . once, when I lived somewhere else, in a foster home," Christopher said. Then he changed the subject abruptly. "Come on, climb up."

Lacey stood where she was. In the dark, despite the moonlight, she couldn't read his expression, whether it was serious or joking.

"Come on, we haven't got all night," he said.

"This is crazy. If anyone finds out we've done this . . ." Lacey objected but she climbed up behind him. It felt odd to be sitting there high above the ground. She couldn't see anything but Christopher's back. He squeezed the mare and she set off at a swinging walk. The air was cool. They moved in and out of moon shadow. A screech owl called from the woods up on the hill. It sounded almost like a shrill horse's whinny.

"You'll have to hold on. We're going to trot," Christopher said over his shoulder. Lacey didn't have time to be scared. She held onto his waist. The mare moved ahead briskly. The trot was bumpy but she tried to keep herself balanced. Christopher didn't seem to be having any trouble.

"How many times have you ridden this horse?" she demanded.

"A few," he replied matter-of-factly.

They made a circuit of the field before Christopher slowed the horse to a walk again.

"Isn't it neat? It's like being free, like flying," he said.

"I've always drawn pictures of horses, but I never rode one."

"Is this better than drawing pictures?" he said, looking over his shoulder. She nodded.

From the field they could see the dark bulk of the Snows' house and two windows shining yellow with light.

"Have you ever been in his house?" Lacey asked.

"No."

"I have. My mother worked for them once, cleaning, and I got to see it. It's so beautiful. The woodwork is all oak, and it's smooth and polished. The ceilings are real high with this fancy flowery pattern. And there's a big curved staircase," she said with a flourish of her hand. "I'd love to have a house like that."

"Is that what you daydream about?"

"Sure. Why? What do you dream about?"

"I don't know," Christopher said wistfully. "I guess I'd just like to have a home. I don't mean a house. I mean like having my own family, some place I could always come home to."

"Well," Lacey said, "your dream might be more impossible than mine."

Christopher let the horse keep walking and Lacey finally said, "Christopher, what happened to you? Why are you a foster child?"

She felt his body stiffen. He stopped the mare and looked down at his hands on the reins. He said slowly, "Don't you think it's better not knowing? Just pretend the McIntoshes are my real parents. You know, a typical happy family. That's what I like to do—pretend I'm someone else."

"Come on, Christopher, you can't pretend. I know *I* can't pretend that Lonzie is really my father. He likes to pretend that, but I can't and I won't."

"He's not your father?"

"No. My mother already had me and my sister when she married Lonzie."

Christopher jumped down off the mare. He reached for Lacey's hand and pulled her off, too. Then he unbridled the mare and let her go. She wandered off until she became another shadow in the grass.

Christopher stood there in the moonlit pasture and regarded her. He looked solemn and pale. Lacey felt she had to break the silence. It was making her uncomfortable because she wondered what he was thinking.

"Are you shocked?" Lacey said.

"Where is your sister?" he asked quietly.

"Lonzie sent her away. She's probably in a foster home now. But I'm going to find her."

"Don't you know where she is?"

Lacey shook her head. "My mother won't talk about it."

Christopher didn't say anything. His dark eyes were liquid and full of pain. She wasn't sure whether he was feeling sorry for her or if he was thinking about his own troubles. Maybe she shouldn't have said anything at all. Maybe she shouldn't have asked any questions. Maybe he was right—it was better not knowing. Christopher stood there a long time, not saying anything until she sensed he was ready to speak.

"But I don't understand. You live in a nice little house. Your mother seems so kind. I just thought . . ."

"The typical happy family, right? *You* were pretending that. You don't know Lonzie—how he spends half his time on poker games and half his money drinking."

"I didn't know . . ." Christopher said awkwardly, "about your sister. Why did he send her away?"

"He told my mother he had no intention of raising two kids who weren't his, one was bad enough. He wanted to get rid of me, too, but my mother wouldn't do it, because I was so young. Since my sister was three years older, she was the one who had to go."

"Oh, Lacey . . ."

Now Christopher was feeling sorry for her. She felt terrible.

"I shouldn't have brought it up. I don't know why I did."

They had walked back to the barn and Christopher replaced the bridle. Now they walked toward the pasture fence.

"I guess," Christopher said, "I guess we have more in common than I thought."

He held the barbed wire for her again and she crawled under. They walked back to her house and stood outside her window. Lacey was glad it was close to the ground so she could climb back in without making a lot of noise.

Christopher said softly, "I'll tell you about me . . . sometime. I just can't talk about it right now."

Lacey looked at him and saw he was smiling slightly, but his eyes were sad, like a deer's eyes.

"You don't have to tell me. Like you said, maybe it's better like this," Lacey whispered and slipped back inside.

She lay on the bed, but she couldn't sleep. She just kept seeing that look on Christopher's face. Something must have happened to him. It must hurt to think about it, just like it made her sad when she thought of Vernal. She felt like she and Christopher had known each other for a long time. It was different from being friends with Callie, she knew that. But she wasn't sure just why. She almost felt they were better friends than she and Callie. But how could that be? She hardly knew Christopher. She fell asleep at last, with those puzzling feelings drifting around inside her head.

Seven

CALLIE came by Lacey's house to walk to school. There was no sign of Christopher. She scolded herself inwardly for being disappointed. Callie seemed pleased and talked all the way to school. Today was the last day of the school year.

"I can't *wait* till school's out today. Want to go down to the river as soon as we're out?" Callie asked.

She didn't seem to notice how quiet Lacey was until she failed to get an answer to her question.

"What's the matter, Lace?"

"Nothing. I'm just tired. Lonzie came in late and woke me up and I couldn't go back to sleep." That much was true, she thought.

Mrs. Baxter, the art teacher, came to their class to hand out some sheets of paper.

"Some of you art students," she said, "might be interested to know that the county fair is having an art show this year. There are categories for students and some cash prizes. First prize is fifty dollars. Anyone who is interested can drop off an entry at the school office any time before July fifteenth."

Lacey saw Christopher in the hall after class had let out.

"What are you going to enter in the art show?" he asked her.

"Come on, I can't enter. I'm not good enough."

"How do you know?"

"You enter, then," she challenged him.

"Look out your window at the sycamore tree tonight," he said mysteriously and dashed away down the hall.

"Wait! What are you talking about?" she called to him, but it was too late. He was out the door of the school. Other students pushed in front of her in their eagerness to leave the building and she lost sight of him. What did he mean? Was he planning to go on another nighttime horseback ride? Christopher was so puzzling.

As she and Callie walked home, carrying the last of their school papers, she was still mulling things over. She kept wondering what had happened to Christopher's family. He acted like he had just decided to forget about them. *She* couldn't forget about Vernal. She had a feeling that Christopher was just trying not to think about his mother or father. In fact, she'd almost bet that he really did want to see them again, no matter what had happened. Maybe together she and Christopher could find Vernal and his parents too. Why hadn't she thought of that before? Christopher was a foster child so he'd know exactly how you got foster parents. He might know things that would help her find Vernal. She didn't even know where to start looking. But Christopher would. She felt a burst of happiness and energy, and started running down the sidewalk.

"Come on, Callie! Race!" she cried.

Callie took off after her, but Lacey easily outran her.

"I swear, Lacey," Callie panted. "First you don't say a word all the way home . . . then you run off . . . and leave me."

Lacey just grinned. She couldn't exactly tell Callie why she felt so happy all of a sudden.

Her mood lasted until evening, and when Lonzie came home she even thought about retracting her promise to herself never to speak to him again. He didn't smell of alcohol so maybe he wouldn't be angry tonight. He sat down and ate nearly a whole platter of fried potatoes at supper and then said, "Aren't there any more? Seems like I never get enough to eat around here."

Her mother scraped the remaining scraps from the skillet onto his plate.

"Chickens are laying good now," she said, "so I'll get more egg money and things won't be so tight."

"You think I can't bring in enough money myself?" Lonzie growled. He stabbed the last piece of potato with his fork. "There was a time when we didn't need no extra money."

"I know, Lonzie. I'm just trying to help out," her mother replied softly.

"Don't need that kind of help. Besides, I can always shoot a rabbit or two up on Snow's hill."

Lacey wished she could say something to defend her mother, but she knew Lonzie would only get mad. She felt like telling him there'd be no need for her mother to sell eggs if he didn't spend so much money at the tavern.

Lonzie slid his chair back roughly from the table, got up and went out on the porch. He just stood there looking out across the street, hands in his pockets.

Lacey went to her room, telling her mother she was tired. She lay on the bed, wondering if Christopher would come when it got dark, like he'd said he would. She heard her mother moving around the kitchen slowly, clearing away the dishes. She listened for the sound of the front door opening, signaling that Lonzie had come back in, but she never heard it. The sun had slipped behind the hills on Snow's farm, and the sky turned first rose and then deep blue.

Lacey listened to the train whistle's sad, drawn-out sound and heard the train's faint rumbling grow louder as it approached Milltown. She could tell by counting the whistles exactly where the train was: the first one she heard had to be in Marengo, five miles away. Then there was the crossing on a dirt road near an imposing brick farmhouse, about a mile from Milltown. The next one, pretty close, would be the crossing just outside of town. Then the train would come roaring through town, past the abandoned depot, the whistle blowing hard and loud, drowning out all the night sounds. The clatter and the rumbling seemed to vibrate her bed. She listened as it grew fainter, crossing the river, passing through Brushy Valley and on into the countryside until the sound faded away.

Suddenly Lacey sat up and realized she'd been asleep. She jumped to her feet and looked out the window. Moonlight reflected on something white in the sycamore tree. Carefully she lifted the screen out of the window and climbed out, flinching when sharp sticks and stones touched her bare feet. The white object was a piece of paper, folded neatly in quarters, stuck in the fork of the tree. She opened it up. There was writing on it, but she couldn't read it in the mottled shadow cast by the tree. She climbed back into her room and knelt by the window. She heard another train coming in the distance. She must have slept for some time because the trains didn't usually run very close together. She opened the paper again. A verse was written on it:

> And now the purple dusk of twilight time
> steals across the meadows of my heart.
> High up in the sky the little stars climb,
> Always reminding me that we're apart.
> Sometimes I wonder why I spend the lonely night
> dreaming of a song.
> The melody haunts my reverie,
> And I am once again with you.

The words were so sad and beautiful that Lacey felt like crying. The train had reached Milltown and thundered through the valley. When it had gone, she heard a sound outside. It was Christopher. He came over to the open window.

"Did you like it?" he whispered.

Lacey nodded. "Where'd you get it? Did you write it?"

"It's the words to a song. It's called 'Stardust'."

"It's so pretty," Lacey said.

"Do you want to go for a ride again?" Christopher asked.

In a few minutes they were on their way to the Snows' field. This time Christopher made the mare canter up the sloping field and all around the edge of it. Lacey clung to him. The night wind slid over her face, silky and cool. The mare's canter was smooth and rhythmic, like a rocking chair. When Christopher had slowed the horse to a walk at last, he gestured to the night sky where pinpoints of light glittered. He made a fluttering motion with his hand, as if sprinkling something from the sky.

"Stardust," he said softly. "My mother used to sing that song all the time."

He broke off, as if realizing he'd said something he didn't intend to.

They rode along in silence for several minutes and Lacey decided to broach her question.

"Christopher, will you help me?"

"Help you? Do what?"

"Help me figure out a way to find my sister."

Christopher drew his breath in sharply.

"What's wrong?" Lacey asked, alarmed. She'd turned it over so many times in her mind that her decision seemed matter-of-fact to her. It hadn't occurred to her that he might be surprised. "I thought you'd know all about those kinds of things. I mean . . . you're a foster child. You'd know what they have to go through and everything."

Christopher cut her off. "Yeah, I know what they have to go through, all right." His voice seemed distant and bitter. He pulled abruptly on the reins and jumped down from the mare's back. This time he didn't help Lacey down, but walked quickly beside the mare, holding her bridle. Lacey jumped down on her own. She almost tripped and ran to catch up with Christopher, who was leading the mare away.

"I thought you'd know how to find her better than I would, that's all," Lacey said, trying to explain.

"Oh, sure, I know all about the procedures, the agencies, the social workers. You name it, I know about it."

Lacey could see his profile and his face looked hard and set. His mouth was a tense straight line. She swallowed and her throat hurt. She hadn't expected him to react like this.

"I thought you'd understand . . ." Lacey went on. "I was sure you'd know how important it is to me. And the song . . . I felt like we had something special between us, like I've known you for a long time. We don't have to talk about it, you know? It's just there."

Christopher pulled on the mare's bridle and she halted. He looked at Lacey and there was a painful expression on his face.

"So what did you expect me to be able to do?" he said sharply.

"Just tell me where to start looking."

"Well, I can't help you. I can't help you at all." He avoided her eyes and stared at the ground. "Oh, Lacey, I'm sorry."

He undid the mare's bridle. They walked in silence back to the barn, and Lacey waited while he slipped inside to hang it up. She didn't know what to say, so she didn't say anything. Then they walked back through the damp grass of the meadow. When they got to her house, Christopher left her outside the bedroom window. He touched her hand briefly and gave her a bewildered look. "I'm sorry," he whispered, then turned and walked away.

Lacey lay face down on her bed and let tears run down onto her pillow. She had done something to make him angry or sad and she wasn't even sure what. She lay awake a long time, trying to figure out what went wrong. She had been so sure of Christopher's feelings. She had counted on him to help her. When the next train came through that night, the rhythm of its rattling put her to sleep.

Eight

A week had gone by since Lacey had seen Christopher. Now that school was out, it was warm enough to set out tomato plants and green peppers. Lacey helped her mother in the garden on a sunny morning. She didn't mind digging holes for the young plants, working her hands through the soil. The earthy smell was pleasant and the sun on her back felt good.

"I should have got these out a week ago," Lacey's mother said. "But maybe it's just as well to wait until it's sure not to frost."

Lacey didn't reply. Her thoughts were occupied with Christopher. How would she get a chance to see him again, now that school was out? Maybe she should go to his house. But she felt a little flush of embarrassment at that thought. What if Callie or someone else saw her? Surely Callie would make fun of her and she would probably act jealous, too. In her absentmindedness, Lacey broke the stem of one of the tomato plants.

"Lacey, be careful," her mother admonished. "There's nothing wrong, is there?"

"No," Lacey said.

"When we're finished with this, would you walk down to the store and ask Sam Tucker for their vegetable trimmings? They're so good for the chickens."

When Lacey had firmed the earth around the last plant, she stood up and brushed dirt off her hands. Then she took the bucket that sat beside the door to the chicken house. She didn't mind the task. The only thing she hated was seeing anyone she knew at Tucker's store. Trimmings were free chicken feed, and she knew Mr. Tucker gave them to her mother because he felt sorry for her and knew how unreliable Lonzie was with money. It was almost like begging, she thought.

Lacey scuffed her shoes along the sidewalk as she headed toward the store. When she went inside the grocery, several people were lined up at the counter. Hollis was sitting on an upturned crate, sipping a soft drink. He gave her a blank stare, swallowed the last of it and got up to leave. Lacey stood off to one side, holding the bucket in front of her. Mr. Tucker looked up from the cash register, caught her eye and nodded toward the rear of the store. The people who were lined up saw her then, but Lacey avoided looking at them and strode quickly to the back of the building through a door to the storeroom. There was a cardboard box filled with cabbage leaves trimmed from the heads, carrot tops and some half-rotted potatoes. The carrot greens gave off a sweetly pungent odor.

Lacey scooped them up into the bucket, went back into the store and made a detour behind one of the aisles. She could get back out the door without anyone seeing her, she thought. It was at that moment that Callie spotted her.

"Lacey, what're you doing?" she exclaimed.

Lacey felt hot and flustered, and her bucket of vegetable trimmings seemed suddenly very heavy and large. Why couldn't Callie be quieter? Now she was sure everyone had seen her.

"Want to go down to the dam and swim?" Callie asked.

Lacey shook her head and nodded at her full bucket. "I have to get home."

Callie shrugged. "Okay. If you don't want to, it's okay."

"C'mon, Callie," Lacey pleaded. "Don't be like that."

Callie shrugged again and turned away from her. She headed down another aisle, pretending to be interested in a shelf of bread.

Lacey, lugging the big metal bucket, went out the door without even looking at anyone. She headed up the hill in the opposite direction from where she'd come. She would go home by a different route. She'd walk to the top of the hill where the town dump stood on the lip of one of the old quarry holes. She could walk around the edge of the quarry to get home instead of going up the main street. That way she wouldn't have to contend with people who might stare at her.

She was out of breath when she reached the dump. The rusty, bent metal trash boxes sat on a flat piece of land on the edge of a sheer drop into the old quarry. When this hole had yielded all the limestone it could, Snow's quarry had moved on to another site. It was like a big valley now, with high cliffs on all sides. Its floor was filled with jumbled slabs of limestone. Trees had sprung up between the huge stones and honeysuckle vines had crept across their surfaces. A figure bent behind one of the huge containers, poking through spilled trash with a stick. As she walked closer she realized it was Christopher.

Lacey switched the bucket from one hand to the other because its wire handle was biting into her palm. Christopher turned when he heard her approaching and came toward her.

"What are you doing?" Lacey asked.

"Collecting pop bottles."

Lacey half-smiled and gestured to the bucket. "I guess we're both after trash."

He grinned. When he did that, his eyes were so bright and lively.

"I'm going to turn them in for money to help with your Missing Sister Fund."

Lacey didn't know what to say. "But . . . you said you couldn't help me."

He grinned again and shrugged. "I know. I didn't really mean it."

Lacey just stood there with the bucket in her hand. Christopher pointed at it.

"Were you bringing that stuff here?"

"No. I got it for the chickens . . . down at the store," Lacey said, flustered. "I was just going to walk home this way."

"Well, I was just going to take my bottles and turn them in at the store. Walk back down with me and I'll buy you a Coke."

They sat on the long wooden bench outside the grocery store. The Cokes were fizzy and slushy with ice because Mr. Tucker kept the soft drinks in an old cooler that was too cold. But they tasted good. Voices drifted outside to them through the screen door. Mr. Tucker always kept the doors open in warm weather.

"It ain't right, I say," a man's voice said in a critical tone. "People who can't get food no other way has got a right to hunt."

"Lot of people don't feel that way about their land," they heard Mr. Tucker saying.

Another man's voice entered the discussion.

"I heard it was Snow's son talked him into puttin' up those signs. He don't even live around here. He don't know what he's doin'."

"It just won't work around here. People that has to hunt will hunt just the same. They've been shootin' rabbits and squirrels up on that big hill as long as I can remember. They won't stop now, signs or no signs," the first voice said.

"Who's he gonna get to enforce it?" asked the other man.

"I heard crazy old Hollis was keeping watch on things," said another voice and they all laughed.

One of the voices said, "If Snow lets him wander around on that hill, somebody'll get killed—if he doesn't shoot himself, that is." The discussion broke up as the men left the store.

Lacey swallowed the last of her Coke and stood up.

"I'd better get back with these trimmings," she said.

They both set their empty bottles down beside the bench and began walking up the hill toward home again.

That night Lacey saw another piece of paper in the fork of the sycamore tree. There was no sign of Christopher when she crept outside to get it. She unfolded the paper when she got back inside. Standing near the window, she squinted to read it in the dim light.

It said, "You should enter the art show at the fair. I know you can win. Just think how much that prize money would contribute to your Missing Sister Fund."

Lacey climbed into bed and fell asleep clutching the wrinkled piece of paper.

Nine

WHEN Lacey woke up the next day, the note from Christopher had fallen to the floor. She picked it up and stuffed it into her shoe. She could get rid of it later. She didn't want her mother or Lonzie to see it. When she had finished feeding the chickens, she asked her mother, "Can I go down to the dam?"

"Are you and Callie going to swim?"

"No, I want to take my paper and draw." She paused, figuring she'd have to tell her mother about the fair contest sooner or later. She wouldn't need to tell her why she especially wanted to enter it, though.

"Mrs. Baxter said there's going to be an art show at the fair and I want to enter it. I have to make some really good drawings."

Her mother smiled at her briefly, as if she were proud. "That's nice, Lacey. You go ahead. When you come back, just be quiet. Lonzie's asleep."

He was sleeping because he came home drunk, Lacey thought. He'd be late for work but her mother wouldn't wake him up. She'd probably call and tell the quarry foreman he was sick or make some other excuse. Lacey wanted to slam the door and walk out, whether it would wake Lonzie or not. But instead she left quietly and she knew she'd come home quietly, too.

When she got down to the dam, she found a spot along the riverbank next to some bushes where she could sit on a rock and stay out of the way of the kids who were swimming.

Lacey took out her anger toward Lonzie on the paper, sketching in swift, bold strokes, pressing hard with the pencil. She started by drawing a horse running. She could almost feel the power of the horse's stride. Then she drew hills in the background and realized the scene looked like Snow's field where she and Christopher had ridden. Without thinking about it, she added a boy and girl riding the horse. She turned the page of the sketchbook. She didn't feel so angry anymore.

Now she drew the scene from where she sat—the big red barn perched on the hill across the river with the dam below it where the water rushed over the edge, all frothy. It was a nice picture, she thought. It seemed to capture the feeling of summer. She omitted the kids swimming in the calm pool upstream from the dam. They intruded on the peacefulness of the scene. Suddenly she felt as if someone was looking at her. She turned around. It was Christopher. He was smiling and he had a smug look on his face.

"You took my advice."

Lacey felt herself turning red. She was sure her face was the color of the barn across the river.

"Well, I'll . . . I'll see how it comes out." She gestured to her drawing pad.

He came closer and studied it. "It's terrific!" he said and his voice was genuinely enthusiastic. "I like it. It really looks like a summer day. Are you going to enter this one in the fair?"

Lacey was sure she was much redder than the barn now.

"I was going by here on the way to work," Christopher said, as if making an announcement.

"Work? What do you mean?"

"I've got a job—cutting grass. It pays better than collecting bottles. And everything I earn I'm giving to you—for your Missing Sister Fund."

Lacey's mouth came open in surprise. "Oh, Christopher, really?"

"Sure. You asked me to help. I'm going to try. You might need some money before we're through. Research can be expensive."

Christopher sat down beside her. He clasped his hands around his knees and stared out across the river.

"Do you remember *anything* that could help us find your sister?" he asked.

Lacey thought hard. Then she half-smiled.

"I remember I heard my mother saying Vernal would go to a foster home and I thought that must be a relative because my name is Foster. That's silly, isn't it?"

She looked over at Christopher and found him gazing intently at her. They both smiled and looked down.

Lacey began again, "You know, one day a couple of years ago, I was bringing the mail in and there was a letter with a funny-sounding name on it. When my mother saw it, she right away put it in her purse. I asked who it was from and she said, 'Oh, nobody important.' I kind of wondered if it had something to do with Vernal."

"What kind of a funny name was it?" Christopher asked intently.

"It had something to do with weather. And I think it started with a W."

"Do you remember where it was mailed from?"

"It was West Fork, I think. That's what was so odd about it—all those W's."

"Where's West Fork?"

"Oh, it's down at the other end of the county—it's quite a long ways from here."

"Well, all we have to do is look in the phone book. Maybe if you looked at all the names under W you'd remember it."

Lacey shook her head. "No, it's not in our phone book. That's long distance from here. Everything beyond English is long distance."

Christopher bent his head, staring at the muddy riverbank. Lacey waited for him to say something.

"Someone around here must have that phone book," he said at last. "Let's just think . . . do you think they'd have one down at the store?"

Lacey looked alarmed. "I can't go in there and ask Mr. Tucker for it. Everyone would see me and they'd all try to figure out what was going on."

"Well, I'll do it, then," Christopher said, jumping to his feet. He rubbed his hands against his pants to dislodge the dirt.

"Wait . . ." Lacey said, putting her drawing pad on the ground and standing up. "What good will it do for *you* to look at all those names?"

"I'll write down all the ones under W that sound like weather. There can't be *that* many. See you later."

Christopher strode off in the direction of the store, turned once and flashed her a quick smile.

Could she really be that close to finding Vernal? Lacey wondered. What if she called those people and Vernal *was* there? What would she say? Suddenly the whole idea frightened her. What if Vernal didn't remember her? What if Vernal didn't *want* to talk to her or see her. She wanted to call after Christopher and tell him to wait. Instead, she swallowed a couple of times to loosen her tight throat muscles, picked up her sketchpad and pencil and began walking home. When she got to the hill by the grocery store, she wanted to dash inside and see whether Christopher had gotten the phone book. But she forced herself to slowly start up the hill toward home. She didn't even glance in the store window to see if Christopher was standing at the counter. She was almost home when she saw Callie walking down the street toward her. Lacey wasn't sure if she wanted to talk to Callie right now, but there was no way to avoid it.

Callie wanted to see the drawings. She grabbed the sketchbook and leafed through it quickly, stopping at the picture of the horse galloping through the field.

"Who's this on the horse?" Callie asked.

"It's just a picture. It doesn't have to *be* anyone," Lacey said defensively.

"Looks like it could be you and Christopher. I thought you were the one who didn't want to get married."

"What do you mean by that?"

Callie didn't acknowledge the comment, but went on. "Now you're drawing all kinds of romantic pictures." Callie handed the sketchbook back to her.

Lacey knew she was blushing again. "Who said anything about marriage? Christopher's just my friend. Is there anything wrong with having a boy for a friend?"

"You're always together. *We* used to be best friends. I think you like Christopher better than you do me."

Lacey shot her a look. It was like Callie knew what had been going through her mind. She didn't like the fact that Callie had gotten so close to the truth. They walked on in an awkward silence.

"Well," Callie said stubbornly. "You'll have to make up your mind. We can't both be your best friends."

"Callie, don't say that. Come *on.*"

Callie set her lips together and wouldn't look at her.

"I can't pick one of you. That's stupid!" Lacey exclaimed.

"Just forget it, then," Callie said and her voice quavered. She pursed her lips even harder and walked quickly away, leaving Lacey behind on the sidewalk in front of Lacey's house.

"Cal—wait!" Lacey ran after her but Callie wouldn't stop. She walked briskly down Snow's Row toward her own house.

Lacey was shaking with anger and confusion. Okay, she thought, let Callie be that way. It made her angry and a little afraid, too, but she wouldn't let Callie know that. Callie could ignore her and give her the silent treatment. Well, she'd give it to her right back. But she wondered, was Callie right? *Did* she like Christopher better?

Lacey walked up the steps of her front porch. Why was everything so confusing? Why did Callie have to act like she was jealous? She felt divided between Callie and Christopher and didn't know which way to turn. She stood on the porch, gazing down Snow's Row but not really seeing anything because her feelings were bouncing around inside her head. All of a sudden she heard a voice behind her.

"What's up?" It was Christopher. He walked toward her with a folded piece of paper in his hand.

"What's up is that Callie is mad at me and it's because of you." Lacey's voice was unintentionally accusatory and then she saw the look in Christopher's eyes and she was immediately sorry she'd said it. "But I don't care," she said fiercely. "You're a better friend than Callie is, anyway."

Christopher looked at her seriously and said, "You're a good friend, too, Lacey."

He stood there quietly. "I think you're really the first person who's cared much about me at all. I've always tried to make friends by acting kind of crazy. It just never has worked very well."

"You mean like making up stories about the horse that got run over?"

A little smile crossed his face. "You figured out that wasn't true, huh? I guess it wasn't such a good story."

He looked down then and saw the sketchbook in her hand, turned to the drawing of the horse running. Lacey wasn't sure she wanted him to see it, but it was too late. She watched his face. A strange look came over it when he realized what she had drawn.

"That's you and me," she said. "Do you like it?"

Christopher seemed to be struggling with his feelings. "I like it very much," he said softly.

"Do you think my pictures are good enough for the art fair?"

"Lacey—they're beautiful."

They stood there awkwardly for a minute. Then Christopher, as if he suddenly remembered why he'd come, quickly unfolded the piece of paper. He held it up triumphantly.

"I got the names from the phone book!" he whispered.

Lacey looked behind her nervously at the screen door. "Let's not look at them here. Let's go out by the chicken house."

They walked around behind the house. Lacey looked back and saw her mother at the kitchen window. She waved. She didn't want her mother to think she was hiding something. And she didn't know if Lonzie was still home.

"We'll just sit here," Lacey said, indicating a soft grassy spot in full view of the house.

Christopher nodded. "If your mother comes out, we'll stick the list in your sketchbook. We'll just pretend we're looking at your drawings."

Christopher opened the paper and laid it on the open sketchpad. Lacey studied the list. Christopher was right. There weren't very many names that began with a W that had something to do with the weather. She read the list of names.

Waterford
Waters
Weathers
Wettnight

Whitefield
Windford
Winters

Christopher had also written phone numbers down beside each one. Lacey read through the list two or three times. Then she said quietly, "It's Wettnight. I'm sure of it. I remember it being a really odd name. The rest of the names aren't that unusual."

They sat in the grass and Lacey fingered the sheet of paper.

"Now you should call them," Christopher said calmly.

"What would I *say?*" Lacey exclaimed. She suddenly felt she wanted to abandon the whole idea. It was too hard.

"Just say, 'I'm calling about Vernal.' "

"Oh, Christopher, I *can't,*" Lacey protested. She shut the sketchbook. She had dreamed about seeing Vernal again for so long, but now that it seemed like a possibility, she was scared.

"I can't call from home anyway. It's long distance. I'd have to do some explaining if I did that. I can't call from the pay phone down by the store without the whole town finding out about it."

Lacey stood up and headed back toward the house. Christopher followed her.

"Hey, I'll help you, don't worry," he said. "*I* can make the phone call. I'll be back tonight."

He set off down the street, pausing to turn and wave. Lacey went inside. Her mother was putting two plates on the table.

"Who was that?" her mother inquired.

"Christopher. A friend from school," Lacey answered.

"I don't recall seein' him around town before," her mother said.

"He's new here. He came here just before school was out," Lacey said. She noticed then that her mother had set only two plates on the table. And it was early to be eating supper.

"Lonzie's not home?" she asked.

"No," her mother said without looking up. "He went to work late this morning, so he's staying longer this evening."

Lacey knew as soon as her mother said the words that they weren't true. No doubt he'd gone into work late, but she could tell by the way her mother pressed her lips together that she knew Lonzie wasn't going to stay late at the quarry. She knew he would probably leave work and go out playing cards and drinking and losing all his money instead of making some. Lacey knew that's what he was doing, and she knew her mother knew and it made her angry. But there was no use wishing things would change. So Lacey swallowed her anger as she quietly ate her supper.

Ten

WHEN Lacey was through with supper and helping her mother in the kitchen, she went into her bedroom. She sat on the edge of the bed, waiting for it to get dark, waiting for Christopher. She got her drawings out and looked at them. She wondered if they really *were* good enough for the art show. Time passed slowly as the sun slipped lower in the sky. Finally, at dusk, she heard a noise outside the window. She dropped the sketchbook onto the bed. Christopher lifted the screen out for her and set it quietly back in when Lacey was outside.

"I want to walk over to the quarry. It's a nice spot to sit and talk," he whispered. He started walking away from the house and Lacey followed him.

"What do you want to talk about?" she asked.

"Me." He looked at her with his familiar half-smile, as if waiting to see what she'd say.

"Oh," was all Lacey could say. She wasn't really sure she wanted to hear what he had to say.

It was only about two blocks to the edge of the abandoned quarry. One of the streets dead-ended there, and the last house on the street was several hundred feet from the lip of the quarry. They sat down on a rock overlooking the big gaping hole. The sheer limestone sides of the hole were whitewashed in moonlight.

"So, you wanted to hear my life story. I'll tell you," Christopher began.

"Oh, Christopher, if you don't want to, please, I don't care."

"I *want* to tell you, Lacey," Christopher said, then sighed as if resigned to it. "I grew up in the city, mostly. We never had any money. My father worked in a factory, but he got laid off and never got his job back. He worked when he could get odd jobs. My mother was real smart; she went to college once. But she's crazy now; at least that's what they say. She's in a hospital. That's why I got sent away. My father wasn't working and my mother was 'unfit.' That's what they called it. Before my mother went to the hospital, my father sometimes took off for a couple weeks at a time and left us alone. Once she tried to kill herself."

Christopher stood up and walked to the edge of the quarry, his back to her, as if by not facing her he could talk easier.

"I know she wasn't happy. I tried to talk to her, but somehow it never worked. She'd take spells, you know, and cry, or sometimes just lie in bed for hours. I'd try to talk her out of her spells. Sometimes it worked and sometimes it didn't. I just wanted to be able to do something."

Christopher broke off talking and paced back and forth along the edge of the rocky bluff. Then he picked up a rock and threw it as hard as he could. Lacey heard it strike stone somewhere far below them.

"I don't know why it didn't work the last time. Maybe I just didn't try hard enough," he said and his voice was shaking.

"Christopher, you know it wasn't your fault."

"I try to tell myself that." He turned around and stood facing her. He ran one hand over his eyes and Lacey could see there were tears. She just sat there, still as the moonlit stones. Christopher seemed to be waiting to say something else.

"That was three years ago that I got sent to the first foster home," he continued. "I didn't want to go. As bad as it was at home, at least it *was* home."

"But wasn't it better in the foster home?" Lacey asked.

"The trouble is, you never know how long you're going to stay. You find that out real fast," he said bitterly. "The place I went first was nice enough and the people were real nice, but I was only there three months and they decided they didn't want to be foster parents anymore.

"So what happens to me? I got sent off to another one. I decided I'd act real obnoxious. I was hoping they'd say I had to go home. Instead, I went to another foster home. That was the Duncans. They were real nice people. They lived in the country. That's how I had a chance to learn to ride. A farmer down the road had horses. He even let me use one of them as my special horse, to ride any time I wanted."

"The horse that got run over?" Lacey reminded him, remembering his outlandish tale.

Christopher grinned for a second, then sobered. "That horse *did* die one day. The farmer just found it lying there dead in the field. I don't like to think about it. Anyway, the Duncans worried about me because I didn't do too well in school and I wouldn't talk to them very much. They kept telling me, 'We care about you, Christopher.' I guess I didn't believe it. I mean, what was I *supposed* to say? I couldn't say to them, 'Well, I don't care about *you*.' I knew I'd get sent somewhere else eventually, so what good does it do to care about anyone?"

He shrugged. Then he looked over at Lacey and said guiltily, "I'm sorry. I don't mean that about *you*." He picked up another stone, but instead of throwing it, he worked it back and forth in his hand. "I kind of feel like you're different. I mean—when I found out about your sister. It seemed like we had something in common. I guess I figured you'd understand how I felt, sort of."

Lacey nodded. She was afraid to say anything. She was sure she'd burst into tears if she did.

Christopher rubbed the edge of the stone over and over. "See, that's why I wanted to help you. I know what it's like not to have a real home. I know how your sister probably feels, at least."

Lacey swallowed a couple of times. "Why did you come here? Why did they send you to Milltown?"

"They asked me if I wanted to come here. There was a family wanting someone about my age. They thought maybe it would be good for me to try living in the country again—you know, a better environment than the city. I figured it wouldn't matter, so I didn't object. Let's walk, okay?"

Without giving her time to answer, Christopher started down the path that ran around the edge of the quarry. The moonlight through the leaves made jumbled patterns on the ground. They walked a long way, all around the edge of the big stone pit.

"It *is* beautiful here, you know? You can smell the trees and the grass. Not many places you can do that in the city," Christopher said wistfully.

They walked farther. They heard the shrill, haunting cry of a screech owl.

"I don't want to leave," Christopher said.

Lacey looked at him. She could hardly stand the look in his eyes, like some sorrow that was hidden down deep in them had come to the surface.

"Maybe you won't have to," Lacey said, but she knew her tone wasn't very convincing. The fear suddenly went through her that Christopher might have to leave here and be sent to another foster home. She hadn't even thought about that before.

"I don't want you to leave, either," Lacey said impulsively.

Christopher gave her a quick smile.

Eleven

CHRISTOPHER and Lacey walked back toward the little frame houses on Snow's Row. Lacey hadn't kept track of the time and she wondered how long they'd been gone. They came around the side of their porch and stopped there.

"Oh, I almost forgot," Christopher said. "This is from cutting grass." He reached into his pocket and handed her fifteen dollars. "Three lawns."

Lacey took the money and folded it in her hand. They were just about to go around to Lacey's window when the light snapped on. Christopher hung back and pulled Lacey toward him by the hand. Lonzie stood in the harsh white light from the porch bulb, looking pale and angry. She knew he was drunk, but there was nothing unusual about that. Still, she shrank from him.

"Don't you run off from me!" Lonzie shouted. "Do you know what hour of the night it is? It's eleven o'clock! How long have you been out runnin' around with *him?*" He jerked his head in Christopher's direction. "How long? Answer me!"

Lacey looked at Christopher, her eyes pleading with him to help her, but there was nothing he could do. He looked scared. His face had turned white and he was shaking.

"You have some nerve sneaking back here with him," Lonzie said loudly. He came down off the porch and the smell of alcohol turned Lacey's stomach. He grabbed her by the arm to drag her up on the porch and the money fell from her hand.

"Where'd you get this?" he shouted, shaking her.

"Christopher . . ." she whispered, then stopped short. She couldn't tell Lonzie why Christopher had given her the money. But she didn't have to say anything. He had already drawn his own conclusion. Her answer had filled Lonzie with rage.

"Why'd he give you money? Tell me! Why'd he give it to you?" Lacey still couldn't say anything. She felt like she was frozen to the spot. "You don't take money for being with any boy! Pull cheap tricks like that around here and you won't be in my house much longer."

Lonzie let go of her and stepped toward Christopher, who hadn't moved since the moment the light had gone on.

"I never want to see you around here again, do you hear me?" Lonzie hit Christopher hard in the face, and the blow nearly knocked him down. Christopher backed away with an anguished, helpless expression on his face. Lacey knew he wanted to say something or do something to help her, and couldn't. She wanted to say she understood, but she couldn't. Lonzie pulled her up on the porch and pushed her into the house. Her mother was inside, sitting on the edge of the sofa, with her arms clasped tight to her body, rocking back and forth.

"Lonzie," her mother pleaded. "Lacey didn't do anything."

"She knew what she was doing," he said sharply and pushed Lacey into her room. She heard him leave the house, slamming the door.

Lacey picked up the pillow from her bed and threw it across the room. It hit the dresser and when it did, it scattered a sheaf of torn papers. Lacey saw that the papers were the drawings she had done for the art show, ripped into pieces. She felt like her insides had been torn into pieces, too. How could Lonzie have done that? She was almost too angry to cry. She picked up her hairbrush off the dresser and threw it against the floor. It broke into two pieces and when it did, something inside her broke too and tears flooded her eyes. She fell back on the bed and let the sobs come, until her whole body was shaking.

Her mother opened the bedroom door and came in. She didn't turn on a light.

"Lacey . . ."

"I hate him! I never want to see him again. I'll leave here and never come back!"

"Lacey, you know you don't mean that," her mother said, silhouetted in the doorway. "Lonzie didn't mean those hateful things he said. He just had a little too much to drink. He just doesn't want to see you get in trouble."

"He doesn't understand at all! Christopher and I didn't do anything. We went for a walk, so Christopher could tell me . . . how he got to be a foster child . . . just like Vernal is right now," Lacey said and her throat was so tight she could hardly catch her breath. She glanced at her mother to see if that statement got any reaction and saw a guilty, anguished look flash across her mother's face. Her mother shook her head sadly and pushed a strand of hair away from her eyes.

"So long ago . . . but you've never forgotten, have you, Lacey?" her mother said.

She sat down on the bed beside her and Lacey found she couldn't keep herself from crying harder, as all the anger she had buried came to the surface again.

"I just want to see Vernal again—and I *will*! I *will* find her. Christopher will help me," Lacey said fiercely. "I don't see why you had to let Lonzie send her away."

Her mother slipped a hand over Lacey's and held it gently.

"I know you can't forgive me. I can't forgive *myself*," her mother said in a quiet, strained voice. Lacey could see only the outline of her mother's face in the light from the doorway. "But if you could only understand, Lacey. At least I have you. At least I still have *you*."

When she spoke those words, she closed her hand tightly over Lacey's and held on with a strength that was almost painful. The gesture frightened Lacey a little and she glanced at her mother's face, but she was staring straight ahead as if she were far away from the room. Lacey had stopped crying but her eyelids felt puffy and sore from the salty tears. She wanted to tell her mother what Christopher had found out.

"If I *did* find Vernal . . ." Lacey began.

Her mother withdrew her hand.

"No, Lacey, you can't. Some things are better left the way they are, even if they're mistakes."

She got up and left the room, closing the door softly.

Lacey lay there in the dark. Everything seemed impossible now. How could she enter the art show? Lonzie had destroyed the pictures. And he'd taken the money Christopher had given her. She kept seeing Christopher's face, how he'd looked when Lonzie hit him. How could she face Christopher after what had happened? How could she even see him again without Lonzie finding out? Christopher probably wouldn't ever want to see her again anyway, after being humiliated like that. She thought of what he'd said earlier. "What good does it do to care about anyone?" Would the people you cared about always be taken away from you one way or another? Like Vernal? And now Christopher?

An empty, isolated feeling settled in the pit of her stomach, as if something had been torn from inside her. She kept swallowing but it wouldn't go away. At last she fell asleep, exhausted.

Twelve

When Lacey awoke, she still felt tired, as if she'd been awake all night. She wondered if Lonzie had come home or if he'd stayed out drinking. She wondered if he'd spent her money, and that thought made her stomach draw into an angry knot.

"Lacey," her mother called from the kitchen.

Lacey rose slowly and left the bedroom.

"The chickens are laying so well now, I've got extra eggs. Would you take them down to the store and see if Sam will buy them?"

Her mother was wiping the eggs with a damp rag. She placed them carefully in a bucket and handed it to Lacey. She never said a word about last night.

Lacey took the bucket and headed down the street. She studied the sidewalk as she went, not looking up so she wouldn't have to nod or wave to anyone. She was afraid her eyes might still be red and swollen from crying, and she didn't want anyone to see them.

She walked into Tucker's store. As usual, Hollis was sitting on a crate near the door, sipping a soft drink. As usual, he didn't speak. Sam was bagging a customer's groceries, and he said to her without pausing from his work,

"Take the eggs back to the cooler, Lacey. I'll be back in a minute to count them."

Lacey went to the rear of the store and waited. Sadie, an elderly woman who lived on Lacey's street, brought an armful of canned goods to the counter and set them down with a loud plunk.

"Hear about the row at Lonzie Jackson's last night?" Sadie asked. She didn't wait for Sam to answer. "Myrtle told me about it. Said she saw the porch light go on, just as she was going to the kitchen for a glass of milk to settle her stomach. Next thing she knew she heard Lonzie carrying on. I'm surprised the whole neighborhood didn't hear it."

Lacey felt her face flushing with embarrassment. She knew Sadie hadn't seen her. She wished she could just leave the eggs and run out the back door. But there was no back door.

Sadie continued, "I just don't understand what Lonzie was so fired up about."

Another woman's voice joined the conversation. Lacey recognized it as Myrtle's. "I *told* you," Myrtle said impatiently, "his stepdaughter was out there with some boy." As an aside to Sam, she added, "I guess he was giving them heck for being out late."

"Oh, yes, that's right," said Sadie, as if suddenly remembering. Then she frowned in a puzzled way. "Now I wonder who that would have been."

"I *told* you. It was that foster boy who's living with the McIntoshes," Myrtle said, her tone even more exasperated.

Sam had rung up Sadie's order and put the cans in a sack. Myrtle moved to the counter with her groceries. "Well," she said, "no doubt Lonzie'd been at the tavern. I sure do feel sorry for Adelle, having to put up with that. I can't fault her for tryin' to get a father for Lacey, but it's a shame he won't get straightened around."

The two women left the store and Lacey couldn't hear

any more of what they said. Sam came back to the cooler and took the bucket from her. He avoided her eyes. Lacey looked at the floor while he put the eggs into cartons.

"Three dozen today. Here's your money. Anything else you need?"

Lacey shook her head, took the bucket and left the store. She had just turned the corner to start up the hill toward home when she saw Christopher coming up the street. She wasn't sure whether she should pretend she hadn't seen him. She hesitated and he called to her. "Lacey, wait." He ran a few steps to catch up to her.

"Lacey, I'm so sorry," Christopher said. He looked solemn.

"You don't have to be sorry. It's my fault. If I hadn't said anything . . ."

"No, I should have tried to do something. I just couldn't do anything but stand there."

"I know."

Christopher put his hand on hers briefly. "He just didn't understand." He smiled. "Anyway, don't look so gloomy. The art fair's coming. You have that to look forward to."

Lacey whirled sharply and threw the bucket to the ground. It clattered across the sidewalk. "Why'd you have to say *that?*"

"What? What did I say?"

"Lonzie's ruined all my drawings. And he took the money you gave me. He probably went out and got drunk with it."

Christopher's face went almost as pale as it had last night when Lonzie turned on the porch light. Then it turned red with anger.

"Are you going to let him get by with this? Are you going to give up? That's what he wants."

"What do you expect me to do—draw them all over again?" Lacey said angrily. She bent over and picked the bucket up off the sidewalk.

"Yes!" Christopher said defiantly. "Can't you do that? You drew them once. Draw them again."

"Oh, sure, it's real easy. It's not very long til the fair. I'd have to finish them in a couple of days to get them entered in time."

"At least do that one of the dam and the river. That was your best drawing. I just know you'll win something."

Lacey stood quietly for a few moments. Finally, she said stonily, "All right, I'll do it. But I don't know if it'll be any good, this time."

"Don't worry, it will."

Lacey didn't look at him for a few seconds. Then she turned toward him. "If Lonzie sees you around again, I don't know what he'll do."

"Don't worry about that. I'll have to be careful, that's all." Christopher shrugged. "I'd better go. I was on my way to the store to use the pay phone to call the Wettnights and see what I can find out."

Lacey gripped the handle of the bucket tightly. The thought of finding out about Vernal at last made her feel shaky inside.

Christopher must have been able to tell because he said, "Don't worry, I'll let you know what I find out as soon as I can."

Thirteen

By the time Lacey got to her house, her heart was beating as if she'd been running. She'd actually walked the rest of the way home very slowly, trying to calm the thoughts that raced through her mind like the freight trains raced through Milltown. She couldn't stand to wait to hear from Christopher, but at the same time she dreaded it.

Her mother came to the screen as Lacey climbed the porch steps. "Did Sam take the eggs?" her mother asked.

Lacey handed her the empty bucket and the money.

"Good," her mother said and tucked it into a pocket of her dress. She disappeared inside the cool, dark interior of the house.

Lacey went to her bedroom, retrieved her drawing pad from under her mattress and returned to the front porch. She sat down on the steps and opened the sketchbook to a clean page. She sat there thinking quietly for a minute. Christopher's words ran through her head, "At least do that one of the dam and the river."

Lacey began drawing. Slowly she sketched the outlines of the riverbank, the big barn and the flowing water. They were clear in her memory. Then she began filling in—

straight, stark strokes for the rough siding of the barn, gentle shading for the surface of the water, graceful lines for the trees. Surprisingly, she found it easy. Soon she had recaptured the scene on paper. She was so absorbed that she didn't even hear Callie walk up.

"Hi, Lace. Want to go swimming?" Callie asked.

Lacey jumped to her feet, startled, dropping her pencil.

"Oh, Callie. I didn't hear you come up the sidewalk." She clutched her sketchbook tightly.

"Well, want to?" Callie repeated.

Lacey hesitated. She might miss Christopher when he came back to tell her about the phone call.

"I don't know." She couldn't tell Callie the real reason why she didn't want to go. Lacey held out the drawing pad. "I'm making a drawing for the art show at the fair. I have to get it finished."

"Oh, Lacey, you're no fun anymore." Callie frowned. "You just spend all your time drawing. Well, *I'm* going." She turned and stalked down the sidewalk.

Lacey felt as if she were being pulled in two directions at once. Callie and Christopher were both tugging at her feelings, but right now Christopher's pull was stronger. She picked up her pencil and sat down again but she didn't open the sketchpad. She just sat there with all those conflicting feelings churning inside her, like the water that rushed and boiled around the dam when the river was high after a storm. After a few minutes she went back to the drawing, finishing the shading and the details. A few quick strokes outlined some clouds in the sky and it was done. It *was* a good drawing, she told herself.

When she looked up from the paper she saw Christopher coming up the street. She could tell from his expression that he hadn't found where Vernal was. If he had, he'd be smiling.

Without giving Lacey a chance to ask, Christopher said in a low voice, "She's not at the Wettnights' anymore.

She went to another family at English about two years ago. They told me the name," he said, unfolding a scrap of paper. "Byron Jones." Christopher shrugged. "So I guess that's our next step." He acted as if he had expected another setback. "Why don't you write Vernal a letter? That might be easier. You know, she'll have time to think it over. It won't be such a surprise as calling her."

"How do you even know she's still with this Jones family?" Lacey asked. Then Christopher's words began to sink in. "Do you think Vernal won't *want* to talk to me?"

Christopher gave her a sympathetic look. "Oh, Lacey, I just hope you're not disappointed, that's all." He nodded toward her drawing pad. "Were you working on something?"

Lacey opened the sketchbook to the picture of the river and the dam. Christopher's eyes lighted up and he smiled that slightly crooked smile. They were both grinning as if they'd shared a secret.

"It's beautiful, Lacey." He took the pad from her and studied the drawing. "I think you should take it down to the school and enter it right now."

"Really?"

"Yes, I mean it. Come on." He started down the sidewalk toward the school. Lacey ran after him. She knew they'd pass Callie's house. She was glad Callie had gone down to the river and wouldn't see her walk past with Christopher.

They walked into the school. The corridors were dim, cool and quiet. Lacey tried to remember if she'd ever been inside the school during the summer. Their footsteps echoed as they walked up to the office. Christopher hung back.

"I'll wait here," he said.

Lacey went inside. The office secretary, a middle-aged woman, sat at a desk sorting through stacks of papers.

"I have a picture for the art show at the fair," Lacey said softly.

"In that box over there. Mrs. Baxter will be picking them up," said the woman without looking up from her task.

Lacey carefully tore the drawing from her sketchbook and wrote her name and address on the back. She laid it gently on top of the others and slipped out of the office. She smiled faintly at Christopher. He laughed.

"You look like you've just been to the doctor's office. Just forget all about it. Then you'll go to the fair and see a big ribbon pinned to it."

They walked slowly back to Lacey's house. The sweet scent of honeysuckle surrounded them as they passed the schoolyard fence where it grew thickly, twining itself around the wire. Lacey breathed deeply, drinking in the aroma. She plucked one of the blossoms and held it to her nose. The delicate white flowers were stained yellow with nectar.

When they got to her house, Christopher said, "Write a letter to Vernal. Leave it in the tree by your window and I'll mail it for you."

He must have seen the uncertainty on her face, Lacey thought, because then he added, "Okay?"

"Okay," she agreed.

When Lacey sat down later to write the letter, she couldn't decide what to say. She had gone into her room and shut the door.

What if Vernal didn't write back? She couldn't blame Vernal for just wanting to forget about her sister and mother after what had happened. But Lacey knew that if she *didn't* write the letter, she'd never know for sure. And she couldn't stand not knowing anymore. So finally she wrote simply,

Dear Vernal,
    I've missed you so much since you went away and I've always wondered where you were. Mother won't

talk about you, but I know she misses you too. She just can't stand to say it.

I hope you will answer my letter. I want to see you again.

Love,
Lacey (your sister)

She folded the paper, found an envelope and addressed it:

Vernal Foster
c/o Byron Jones
English, Ind.

Then she slipped outside and stuck the letter in the fork of the sycamore. In the morning the letter was gone.

Fourteen

LACEY was helping her mother peel potatoes for supper three days later when Lonzie came home. It was much too early for him to be off work already. Lacey glanced at her mother and saw just a thin shadow of fear pass across her face. Any time something changed, it was always for the worse, Lacey knew, especially when it involved Lonzie. But her mother concealed her feelings and said, "Lonzie, why're you home so early?"

Lonzie went straight to the refrigerator, got a bottle of beer, opened it and sat down hard in the chair. His body dropped into the chair with a creak. He took a big swallow of beer before he said anything.

"Quarry shut down early. All caught up with our orders and there wasn't any new ones, so the boss said we'd just as well go home."

"Oh," Lacey's mother said, as if she weren't sure how she should react and was trying to be careful.

"Just great, ain't it?" Lonzie asked bitterly, setting the bottle on the table with a clink. "Rumor's going around they're going to lay off a bunch of people and this is how they get us used to the idea. A little at a time." He took another swallow from the bottle and said, "What's for supper?"

"I'm going to fry up a pan of potatoes and eggs," Lacey's mother said, almost apologetically.

"Is that *all* I get?" Lonzie demanded. He set the beer bottle down so hard that some of the liquid sloshed out of it onto the table. "I *can* still put meat on the table, you know."

He stood up, strode into the bedroom and came out with his shotgun.

"Lonzie, what're you doin'?" Lacey's mother asked in alarm.

"I aim to go up on the hill and kill us a rabbit or something for supper."

"Lonzie, please don't go there. Not on Snow's hill. You know he's posted it against hunting. Why, if Hollis saw you, there's no telling what he'd do."

"You think I'm scared of that simpleminded fool?" With that, Lonzie left the house, banging the screen door after him.

Lacey's mother wrinkled her forehead with worry, but went on peeling the potatoes.

"Oh, Lacey, I'm just afraid Lonzie'll go get himself killed. But I can't talk sense into him when he's like this," she said.

Lacey finished her batch of potatoes, laid the knife down and walked out onto the front porch. She realized her hands were shaking. Why should she be frightened? After all, the things Lonzie had done to hurt her, why should she worry about him now? She didn't know why, but the thought of Lonzie dying chilled her. She clenched her hands a few times to calm herself. She gazed down the street. As soon as she did, she saw Christopher walking along the street toward her.

"Lacey!" he called out. "Can you go to the fair with me?" When he got closer he must have seen the expression of fear and worry on Lacey's face because he said, "What's wrong?"

Lacey told Christopher what had happened and his dark eyes clouded over with concern. He looked off toward Snow's hill as if concentrating. Then he said, "If we can find Hollis, we can keep him from going up on the hill. Come on, we'll go to the Snows' barn. There's a good chance that's where he is."

"But . . ." Lacey waved toward the interior of the house.

"Tell your mother we're going for a walk," Christopher replied. "Hurry."

Lacey opened the door, glanced at Christopher for re-assurance and disappeared inside. She came back out again quickly. Her mother's voice called out from inside, "Don't go too far, Lacey."

Christopher pointed and said, "We'll go around the block to get to the Snows' pasture. That way your mother won't see us."

They walked as quickly as they could without running. When they got to the pasture, Christopher deftly slipped under the barbed wire fence and held a strand up taut so Lacey could stoop beneath it. Then he set out running toward the barn. Lacey ran after him, not quite able to keep up with his longer stride. The Snows' horses were gathered at the water trough near the barn, dozing in the shade.

When they were halfway across the field, a loud bang sounded from the woods on Snow's hill. Christopher ran faster and Lacey tripped in the grass trying to catch him. He ran on and then stopped abruptly. He pointed, panting for breath. "Look!"

A figure was headed from the barn toward the hill. From the man's slightly stooped appearance they knew it must be Hollis. The man stopped and set something down against a fencepost while he opened a gate. As if in a hurry, he didn't bother to close the gate behind him. He strode quickly up the hill.

Christopher leaped forward again. In a few seconds he was at the barn, but instead of heading toward the open gate, he disappeared around the corner of the building. Lacey cried, "What are you doing?"

She stopped to try to catch her breath. It was coming so fast and hard, her throat hurt. The exertion had brought tears to her eyes. Christopher reappeared with a bridle slung over his shoulder.

"I'm going to ride one of the horses. I'll never catch up to Hollis on foot."

Christopher walked up to the horses and they turned toward him in curiosity, pricking their ears forward with interest. He slipped up next to the brown mare with the white star, the same horse they had caught on their night-time ride, grabbed hold of her mane and slung the reins over her neck. He fastened the bridle quickly. Then he led the mare to the wooden gate, climbed up on the boards and leaped to her back.

"Come on," he called to Lacey and held out a hand.

When she hesitated, he said, "Climb up on the gate." Lacey did what he said and Christopher pulled her onto the mare's back.

"Just hold onto me tightly," he instructed. She clasped her arms around Christopher's waist and he urged the mare on. She trotted for a few strides and Lacey was sure the jerky motion would throw her off. But Christopher drummed his heels hard into the mare's sides and she broke into a gallop. The rolling motion of the mare's long strides helped Lacey regain her balance. They galloped up the hill in big bounds. There was no sign of Hollis.

Christopher pulled the mare to a stop on the hilltop at the fringe of the woods. Just as he did so, they heard another shot. The closeness of the noise made the mare jump sideways in fright. There was a strangled cry, as if someone were in pain, then another shot. Then silence.

Christopher pushed the mare forward again, turning into the woods along a wide path that led through the trees. A few feet farther on they saw Hollis standing and Lonzie lying on the ground.

Christopher pulled the mare to an abrupt stop, leaped off and flung the reins around a tree branch. Lacey slid off after him and together they ran forward.

"Hollis, stop!" Christopher cried, holding his hands out toward the man. Hollis, still holding the shotgun aimed at a spot in the trees, turned toward him, his expression blank and his face pale.

"Hollis, please put the gun on the ground," Christopher said slowly and firmly. Lacey watched as Hollis silently obeyed.

Christopher nodded at Lacey to indicate it was all right to go to Lonzie. Lacey ran and knelt next to him. Lonzie was bent over, clutching his side and his leg, his eyes shut tight in pain and a grimace on his face. Lacey could see that his shirt and his pants leg were becoming red with blood. She touched his arm.

Lonzie's eyes came open. He seemed confused to see her there. He clutched her hand as tightly as he could. "Need help," he gasped.

"Hollis, just sit here and wait. I'll go for Mr. Snow," Christopher said. Hollis followed him like a dog and sat down on a stone.

"Mr. Snow knows I was just protectin' his place," Hollis said calmly.

"I'll call for help from Snows'," Christopher said to Lacey. Then he grabbed the mare's reins and swung up onto her back. The horse galloped down the path and out of the woods.

Lacey crouched next to Lonzie. He still held onto her hand, but he had clamped his eyes shut again. Lacey didn't know what to do or say. The whole woods seemed so quiet she felt like shouting just to break the silence. Hollis sat on the rock a few feet away, staring straight ahead, as if he were sitting in the woods by himself, thinking peacefully. Lonzie opened his eyes again.

"Are you still there, Lacey?" His voice was strained and low.

Lacey started to reply to reassure him, but reflex halted her and she glanced away. She remembered her promise never to speak to Lonzie again. She had faithfully kept that promise to herself ever since she'd made it that day in the chicken house. Now she looked down at Lonzie. His eyes were still turned upward to meet hers, but they didn't seem to focus on her face. She wondered if he was even aware that she was holding onto his hand. And she wondered what good keeping her promise would do now. Lonzie didn't even know about her secret vow. Likely as not, he'd never even noticed, and her refusal to speak to him hadn't hurt him a bit. But Lacey decided that Lonzie needed to hear her voice right now more than she needed to stick to an angry promise.

"Lacey?" he asked again weakly.

Lacey swallowed hard. "Yes, Lonzie, I'm still here," she said.

"Please don't leave . . ." he said, and his voice trailed off.

Lacey found she couldn't get even one word past her throat to tell him she wouldn't leave. She shook her head fiercely instead and rubbed her eyes with one hand to brush tears away.

Silent minutes passed. She couldn't count how many. Lacey watched the stain creep farther down Lonzie's pants leg and saw it grow larger on his shirt. The ambulance would have to come from Marengo, five miles away. She wondered how long it would take.

Lacey thought she heard a siren and sat up to listen intently. Yes, there it was. The wailing grew louder as it got closer. It would be the ambulance, no doubt, and maybe the town marshal, if Christopher had told the Snows what had happened. Then the siren stopped. The ambulance must have turned off the road into Snows' driveway. She wondered how it would be able to get up the hill.

The next sound was of a straining engine and a vehicle

bumping over the uneven ground of the pasture. Then the engine noises stopped and she heard doors slamming—too many for one vehicle. Then she remembered the town marshal had probably come too.

A group of people rushed into the clearing. Two ambulance attendants rushed to Lonzie's side and turned him over. One began taking his pulse and respiration. Another began applying a tourniquet to his leg. Lacey stood up and moved aside.

Mr. Parkinson, the town marshal, stepped quickly over to Hollis, lifted him off the ground by his shirt and handcuffed him. Mr. Parkinson shook his head as if disgusted. "This never should have happened," he said.

Then Lacey's mother, Christopher and Mr. Snow appeared in the clearing. Lacey had never seen Mr. Snow up close. He was tall and dignified-looking with graying hair.

Lacey's mother was white-faced. "I knew this would happen. I knew this would happen," she said over and over, clenching her hands. She put one palm to her forehead. "I was afraid this would happen all along."

The attendants brought a stretcher from the ambulance, laid Lonzie gently on it and quickly carried him into the vehicle. The ambulance doors slammed shut with a force that startled Lacey and she winced. The vehicle started up and began rolling down the hill. It couldn't go very fast because of the uneven ground.

Mr. Parkinson turned to Lacey's mother and said gently, "We'll get someone to take you over to the hospital later, Adelle, if you want. I don't think there's much you could do just now." Then he turned to Mr. Snow and said angrily, "I warned you about them 'No Hunting' signs. You ought to have known that wouldn't set right with people around here."

Mr. Snow took a step back and an astonished look came over his face. "Certainly you can't blame *me* for this."

"I ask you who told Hollis to patrol this hill with a shotgun?" Mr. Parkinson said.

Hollis looked off into space, not meeting any of their eyes.

"Hollis isn't an employee of mine. I let him sleep in the barn in exchange for keeping an eye on things. I knew he had a gun but as far as I was concerned, that was just a way to discourage people from coming around. I have a barnful of good alfalfa hay and some pretty valuable horses in that field."

The marshal shook his head again. "I'm sorry, Snow, but that's just not how people around here will see things."

"That's right," said another voice. They all turned to see Sam Tucker. He was out of breath from climbing the hill. "As soon as those signs went up, everyone in the store started talkin' about it."

Two other men came up behind Sam. They looked familiar. Lacey guessed she'd seen them at the store. They both nodded in agreement with Sam.

Sam continued, "You just can't take something away that people have considered theirs all this time."

"But *I've* owned this land for years—since I started the quarry," Mr. Snow protested.

"That don't matter a bit. People's been huntin' on that hill since before you were born. They see as they have a right to," Sam said.

One of the other men nodded forcefully. "Sam's right. Why, there's many a family wouldn't have had any other way to put meat on the table when times got hard if they hadn't gotten a little game in those woods and briars on top of that hill."

Mr. Snow's face was flushed with anger, but he was silent.

"People down at the store won't be surprised to hear about this," Sam said. "Why, they were joking about Hollis and how he'd probably set up on that hill and shoot somebody."

Lacey looked at Hollis's face to see if he reacted to the words, but he just continued staring as if he hadn't heard a bit of the argument.

Christopher had been quiet but suddenly he spoke up, glancing from one to the other of the men. "I'm not saying Mr. Snow should have put those signs up. But Hollis wasn't patroling that hill like you're saying. When Lacey and I came across the pasture, we heard a shot fired up on the hill. Then a minute later we saw Hollis come out of the barn and start up the hill. He only went up there *after* he heard somebody shooting."

"Well . . ." said Mr. Parkinson. "Is that how it happened, Hollis?"

Hollis turned his eyes on the marshal's face for a moment, nodded once, and looked away again.

Sam and the other men stood quietly, as if bewildered.

Christopher said, "I don't think Hollis really realized what he was doing. I don't think Mr. Snow really understood, either." He glanced at Mr. Snow, as if to apologize for being critical. He hesitated, then went on. "I mean, everybody in Milltown knows, I guess, that Hollis is, well, kind of simpleminded. He's not quite right and I think he could get confused. Mr. Snow didn't think about how all this could happen. I don't know who to blame."

The marshal, Sam and the two other men looked at each other and at Mr. Snow and Christopher. They all seemed uncomfortable. Finally Mr. Parkinson said, "I guess there's some truth to that. Maybe I did speak too harshly. But Hollis has to be arrested, no matter what. I just hope Lonzie pulls through or there's going to be some mighty upset people in this town." He cast a disparaging glance at Mr. Snow. "It's a messy thing, no matter which way you look at it." He jerked at Hollis's handcuffs and led him toward the car. "It's time we got down off this hill. I can give you a ride, Adelle."

Lacey's mother nodded as she moved slowly toward the car. Sam and the other two men began walking down the hill and Mr. Snow followed, keeping some distance behind them.

Christopher and Lacey stood together silently for a minute, watching the procession descend toward the Snows' house and barn. Then Christopher took her hand and they began walking down the hill.

Fifteen

THE sun had dropped behind the trees on Snow's hill by the time Christopher and Lacey reached the bottom. They walked through the lower fields where the night dampness was already settling in. In the low spots they could feel the coolness of the air. The grass was already tipped with droplets of moisture.

They didn't speak but just walked hand in hand. They slipped back under the barbed wire fence and cut through the little streets to Lacey's house.

As they came up the steps to the front porch, Lacey let go of Christopher's hand. She suddenly felt self-conscious. Light shone through the screen door. Voices and the clatter of dishes came from inside. "Here's Lacey," someone said.

Lacey opened the door and went in. Christopher hung back, unsure, on the porch, until Lacey nodded at him. He followed her inside but stood a few feet away by himself.

Lacey's mother sat on the couch. She rose, went to Lacey and pulled her close with her arms. Lacey laid her head on her mother's shoulder. Then they drew apart and looked at each other. Her mother's eyes glistened and her eyelids were swollen. Her face was splotched with red.

"There's no news yet," her mother said. "Get yourself something to eat." She gestured toward the kitchen. "The neighbors have pitched in to cook us some supper."

Myrtle Roberts was in the kitchen frying pieces of chicken in a skillet. Standing next to her was Sadie, who was washing pieces of chicken and dipping them in flour. Her motions were deliberate. Sadie was slow all around, Lacey thought, from her body to her thoughts. Neither of the women saw her come in.

Sadie said, "But what I don't understand is who sent Lacey up on that hill after Lonzie. No one in his right mind would do that."

"I *told* you, no one *sent* her up there. She just went," Myrtle said firmly.

"Oh yes, that's right," Sadie nodded. She coated another piece of chicken and laid it in the hot grease. The fat spluttered and popped. Myrtle gently pushed the frying pieces aside to make more room in the pan.

"But I just don't understand why anyone would send Lacey up on that hill . . ." Sadie began again.

Myrtle cut her off sharply and said in exasperation, "I *told* you . . ." At that moment, Myrtle turned and saw Lacey standing in the kitchen doorway.

Myrtle smiled apologetically. "I'm sorry, dear, but Sadie's a bit forgetful." She poked at the spattering chicken. "There's a couple pieces of this chicken done now. Why don't you come in and have some?" Myrtle saw Christopher in the living room. "Ask your young man to come have some, too. I'm sure it was quite a shock, finding Lonzie and all."

Lacey pulled a chair out and motioned to Christopher to sit down at the table. Myrtle set plates in front of them. The aroma of the chicken, juicy and hot, made Lacey realize she was hungry.

"There, that'll do you good. Sadie, pour 'em some tea," Myrtle directed. "I had a pot full of these green beans goin' at home, so I just brought them, too," she said, putting a big spoonful on each of their plates. "They're last year's beans but it was a good crop, so I still had a lot left. I don't know *how* many quarts I put up."

Christopher gulped down a big swallow of iced tea, between huge bites of chicken and forkfuls of green beans. Lacey looked across the table at him. She wondered how he'd had the courage to say all those things to the town marshal.

"Lacey . . ." a timid voice said from the kitchen doorway.

Lacey looked up to see Callie standing there, holding a foil-covered pan.

"My mama just baked this chocolate cake this morning," Callie said, glancing first at Lacey and then at the floor. "Well, when she heard about what happened, she told me to bring it over." She set the pan on the table.

Before Lacey could say thank you, Myrtle came around and snatched the foil off the pan.

"Why, tell your mother that's so sweet of her. Sit down, Callie, and eat a piece right now with Lacey and . . ."

"Christopher," filled in Christopher, as he swallowed a mouthful of chicken.

Myrtle got a knife and cut three squares of cake and put down three servings. Callie reluctantly pulled out a chair and sat down. She glanced furtively at both Christopher and Lacey. Lacey's eyes met hers briefly. Callie studied her plate as she carefully cut a piece of cake with her fork.

"I hope Lonzie's all right," Callie said at last.

"We haven't heard anything," Lacey replied, politely but coolly.

"Guess you can't go to the fair tomorrow," Callie said. Her tone was almost a question.

"I guess not," Lacey said. She'd forgotten all about the fair. She and Christopher exchanged looks. She wondered how her drawing had fared in the art show judging.

The phone rang and the sound startled all of them. Lacey looked worriedly toward the living room.

"Oh, dear," Myrtle exclaimed.

"Yes . . . yes," Lacey heard her mother's voice saying. "I'd appreciate that. Thank you very much." Then they heard the click of the receiver. Her mother came to the kitchen door.

"It's all right. That was just Sam down at the store. He's sending us over a nice ham."

"Oh, thank goodness," said Myrtle. "That phone ringing gave me such a fright."

Lacey, Christopher and Callie quietly ate their cake and drank their iced tea.

"More tea, Callie?" Myrtle asked.

Callie shook her head. "No. I'd better go now."

She got up and pushed her chair back under the table.

"Bye, Lacey," Callie said softly. They half-smiled at each other.

Lacey took the plates to the sink and Myrtle took them out of her hands. "Don't you worry with these. Just go sit with your mama, now, honey," Myrtle said.

Lacey went into the living room and sat down on the couch next to her mother. Christopher took a chair on the other side of the room.

"I expect they're operatin' on Lonzie and that's why we haven't heard anything," Lacey's mother said. Lacey nodded.

The three of them sat silently for several minutes. They could hear the sounds of Myrtle and Sadie washing the dishes. The water gushed into the sink and plates and silverware clattered against its surface.

Then Lacey's mother rose and went into her bedroom. Lacey heard a dresser drawer open and shut, and then her mother reappeared in the living room holding a piece of paper in the palm of her hand. She had a strange expression on her face, a mixture of longtime sorrow and determination. She looked at the paper for several seconds, as if gathering strength to speak.

"There's something I want to show you, Lacey. I know now it was wrong of me to keep things from you all this time. I guess I thought what was done was done and there wasn't any changing it. But all the way back to the house this evening, all I could think of was, 'I've got to show this to Lacey.' I guess maybe trouble makes you think about things. Never mind why, I know it's the right thing."

She sat down next to Lacey and handed her the square of paper. It wasn't merely a piece of paper at all, but a photograph. Lacey studied the figure of a slim girl wearing a pale blue dress, photographed against a bush of bright red roses. The delicate face was long and slender. Her hair, hanging thinly about her face, was so pale it was almost white.

"Vernal . . ." Lacey whispered. She looked in wonder across the room at Christopher. A smile spread across his face and his dark eyes glowed as if he felt the same sudden happiness.

Lacey's mother worked her fingers up and down on the hem of her dress.

"That picture was taken two years ago when Vernal went to stay with some new people in English. They sent it to me."

"I knew . . ." Lacey started to say, but her mother went on as if she hadn't heard.

"They told me we could visit Vernal if we wanted, but I was just too stubborn or something. I'd done what I'd done and there was no going back. Lonzie would have thrown a fit, of course, but I could have done it without him finding out. I used to tell myself, 'Now what if Vernal had died? It would be just like this. You couldn't go to see her or ever get her back.' And I thought if I just didn't talk about her, you'd forget her. You were so little, then, I hoped you didn't remember much about it. I hoped you'd forget all about Vernal." Her mother made a little choking sound in her throat.

"I didn't forget . . ." Lacey said softly.

"I know," her mother said and held Lacey's hand. "I used to almost wish Vernal *had* died. I could get over *that* someday. This seems so much worse because in one way I lost her forever but in another way I hadn't. There was just always a little bit of hope. It seems it hurts so much worse this way." Her mother sighed. "I know it was wrong to shut you out of your sister's life."

Lacey traced the edge of the photograph with her finger. She had wondered for such a long time what Vernal looked like now, whether she would recognize her. She needn't have wondered. She'd known Vernal the instant she'd looked at the picture. She couldn't bring herself to tell her mother about finding out where Vernal was, about the letter she'd written. Not just at this moment, anyway.

Her mother let another long sigh escape, as if she'd let go of a very heavy burden. She squeezed Lacey's hand.

"Why don't you and Christopher take a walk? No use sittin' around this house waiting. It's enough to give you a case of nerves."

Lacey nodded and handed the photograph back to her mother. Christopher rose and they stepped out onto the front porch. The night air was cool and damp and heavy with the scent of honeysuckle. They walked out onto the sidewalk. Sounds came to them from the open windows of the neighbors' houses and Lacey heard a whippoorwill call from Snow's hill. Its shrill, lonely cry made her shiver.

"You didn't tell her," Christopher said.

"No, I just couldn't," Lacey answered.

"Vernal will probably get your letter tomorrow."

"I *will* tell her. I just couldn't do it right now. I'll tell her tomorrow."

They turned down one of the streets to walk around the block. Moths fluttered around a street light overhead. The lamplight shining through the trees made dappled patterns of greenish light. They walked without talking but somehow it seemed they didn't need to speak.

As they approached Lacey's house again, they heard a phone ringing inside. Lacey gave an anxious glance at Christopher. He reached for her hand. Lacey was afraid to go inside. The phone had stopped ringing. Faint sounds of voices drifted through the open windows. As they drew closer, Lacey thought she heard Myrtle's voice say, "Thank God."

Lacey and Christopher went up the steps and into the house. Lacey's mother had her hand at her mouth. She shut her eyes briefly and said in relief, "They say Lonzie's going to pull through."

Myrtle put her hand on Adelle's shoulder. The phone rang again, its jangling sound sharp in the quiet room.

Lacey's mother answered it and said, "Yes, just a minute," and then, holding the receiver out, "It's for you, Lacey."

Lacey picked up the phone. It was Mrs. Baxter's voice.

"I'm calling to let you know about the fair contest," Lacey heard her teacher say. She listened a moment and then looked straight at Christopher and said into the phone, "Second place?"

A wide grin spread across Christopher's face.

"Twenty-five dollars? Thank you! And thank you for letting me know."

Lacey put the receiver down softly and realized she, too, was grinning. Christopher leaped from his chair, grabbed Lacey and spun her around in the middle of the room.

"I *told* you!" he exclaimed.

Lacey saw her mother's confused expression and began laughing. The sudden excitement after so much tension made her feel like a tightly wound spring that had just been released.

"I won second place! At the fair—for my drawing," Lacey explained.

Her mother smiled and sank back against the couch. "That's wonderful. I couldn't for the life of me figure out what was going on."

"*And* she got twenty-five dollars for it, too," reminded Christopher.

Lacey's mother shook her head in amazement. "That's a sight better than what I make off selling eggs."

"Except," said Lacey, and she met Christopher's eyes with a subtle smile, "except I guess I won't really be needing that money after all."